Vanishing Point

By the same author:

Poetry
Workshopping the Heart: New and Selected Poems
Swamp Soup (children's poems).
Felis domestica and other poems
The Mother Workshops
House Arrest.
Monster Love
Indian Movies
Death as Mr. Right

Fiction
The Electrolux Man and Other Stories

Fiction for Young People
Riding the Blues
Beyond Blue
Better Than Blue
Mickey's Little Book of Letters
Bruise
Goliath

Children's Picture Books
A Coat of Cats
Swamp Soup
What Goes With Toes?
Beaches
Sunny Faces
You Be the Witch

Critical Books
Research Methods in Creative Writing (ed. with Graeme Harper)
Creative Writing Studies: Practice, Research and Pedagogy
(ed. with Graeme Harper)

Vanishing Point

Jeri Kroll

PUNCHER & WATTMANN

First published in 2015
Published by Puncher & Wattmann
PO Box 441
Glebe NSW 2037

http://www.puncherandwattmann.com
puncherandwattmann@bigpond.com

National Library of Australia
Cataloguing-in-Publication entry:

Kroll, Jeri
Vanishing Point

ISBN   9781922186584

I. Title.

A821.3

Cover Design by Matthew Holt

This project has been assisted by the Australian Government through the Australia Council, its arts funding and advisory body.

Contents

Profile

Statistics

Name: Diana Warren
Age: 19
Weight: 65 kilos
Height: 157 centimetres
Body type: medium
Bones: heavy
Eyes: blue-green
Birthmark: oval on inner thigh
Brother, Philip, 22
Father: Robert
Mother: Lacey

Analysis

Name: Diana Warren
Like the rabbit, she doesn't belong.
'Exterminate, exterminate.'

Age: 19
Going on 90. Sleeps all the time.

Weight: 65 kilos
After power walk.
Lacks self-control at 1 am
in the belly of the dark.

Height: 157 centimetres
Needs to be taller.
Some torture is called for:
bring back the rack.

Body type: medium
Takes after her mother,
the Blob who couldn't eat
just one of anything.

Bones: heavy
Dragging her down.

Hair: sunburnt brown
Fly away, fly away, fly away home.

Eyes: blue-green
When happy. Green near abfab girls.

Birthmark: oval on inner thigh
Pale stain, tiny leaf.
Use to identify body after death.

Goal: A body to match her soul.

Family Breakdown

Philip: Down Syndrome child.
Eternal Care Bear,
sticky with love.

Lacey: born again,
fat with God.

Robert: Master Builder,
demolition expert.

Part One: Losing It

Losing It

I hate things that reflect:
mirrors, windows, pools of water,
father's flashy car,
the eyes of that slim boy
in my old school –
ice blue, ice cool.

They tell me what I already know –
I need more off the hips and thighs
before I can stop.
I need to put what passes
for my life on hold
since losing is the most demanding art.

Term One arrives and so do I,
a virgin student at this place –
fresh start for my new self.
The counsellor checks me out.
I tell her I've begun a fantasy –
creative writing. But that's not the truth.

This is a story
written on my body:
my words made flesh.

'Losing It' is short and sweet,
not like those bloody wars and quests
some gorge on late at night,
with chocolate their best friend,
or tales of greedy sex
and slimy bodies.

I played with the set recipe of
how to be original.
I chose my plot, my character –

she's nothing special,
but her figure is to die for,
or will be soon.

So let me introduce you to my hero.
Begin with the ingredients that matter:
Kilos: 65
Stone: 10.2
Pounds: 143
I'm counting down to zero.

Definitions

I've heard all the names,
know exactly what they mean:
Blimp, Sub, Fat-Arse.
Kirsty the Brick Dunny
has 'a glandular condition'.
She's smaller than Chris, aka Jabba the Hutt.
And me? Short and fat,
Gimli Girl, the crafty dwarf.

Most boys so dim they couldn't find
two words to rub together
to strike a thought —
but Hippo Honey bounces by,
they scan their brains for labels
faster than a checkout chick.
I've learned to match the numbers
with the names.

1– 2 kilos overweight —
no one knows but you.
Do you want a life?
Face the mirror and engage guilt drive.

5 kilos over equals plump —
'pleasantly' only in a parent's eyes.

5 – 10 means on the cusp of fat.
Hear alarm bells ring.

10 and over's courting social death.
Feel the grease on your skin.

10 – 20 kilos? Think obese.
You're off the charts, the radar,
left this planet.
Make friends with the first aliens you meet.

Shapechanger

My parents moaned (no, they're not having sex)
when I dropped out of school.
I wanted to slip through the system's cracks
like mercury, alchemy's first matter,
liquid at room temperature,
aka quicksilver, toxic as vapour.
I remember what I need to know
from that witless kindergarten.

When I enrolled in another college,
my faithful mother thought her prayers were answered.
My sceptic father talked about careers.
Well, they have their agendas, so have I.

Finally I'm on track,
training to vanish in the distance,
with privacy and time
to flow into the form I choose.
Like mercury, revolve in my own orbit,
speed like the god on winged feet,
become the one true message,
conduct my own experiment on me.

Diana, powerful shapechanger,
that's my fantasy.

Static

In my last school
everyone tried to be so cool
they didn't need an air conditioner.

Here it's lukewarm,
maybe because of those like me
not knowing how much energy to give.

But I have plans and visions
that no one here will know until I say.
My mind prepares to drift but then a boy,

a man really, hurries in, sits down,
apart from the main pack.
He doesn't fit this room.

His jeans are worn. A rural logo on his Tee
shows he doesn't try to hide his life.
When he speaks, his voice charms the girls

who ignored me when we chose our seats.
They're dressed to impress:
dangly earrings, short skirts, clingy tops.

'Irish,' they whisper. 'Spunky.'
I wouldn't think a lad on the land
would feed a chick lit fantasy.

Something in the set of his back
suggests that Conor – that's his name –
is more than that. Then someone speaks.

Who? Authority. I click back fast.
Time to harness words
and let my answer trot along,

but his body sticks
at the corner of my eye.
I don't even try to rub it out.

As we jostle through the door
our arms brush.
Does he feel the static?

Biology

I study the living world to know myself —
unhealthy animal that I am,
spirit trapped in so much flesh,
a fly almost fossilized in amber.
Almost.
There's time to change I remember.

I study genus and species —
the plenty of Noah's ark.
Two by two the animals came
into my brother's bathtub boat.
Now I learn what *Homo sapiens*,
dominant till now, has done to them.

What counts? Heredity? Environment?
I'll take my family. They're a good case study.
Colouring: like skin, hair and eyes.
Heart: how well do we keep the beats?
Build: Which parent set my body shape?
Weight: Is any one of us 'just right'?

I'm forced to learn the magic of genetics.
Genes decide who becomes a genius —
or not. There's always accident or fate.
For better or for worse,
they can pronounce life sentences on us.
My family lives this truth.

Numbers

My mother's good with numbers,
trained as an accountant
but dropped out to have Philip.
She keeps my father's books,
and works part-time.
Numbers, family, God – that's her life.

Genetics puts its faith in numbers,
the vital count of chromosomes
at every person's birth.
When the doctors looked at Philip's face
they knew the simple truth –
he wouldn't ever properly add up.

My mother held him in her arms.
There she was, a pretty twenty-three,
staring puzzled at the camera.
Gran insisted on at least one picture.
Dad couldn't see the point –
grandchild or not.

'Whose chromosome's at fault?'
That was the question
Dad asked the doctors.

'You and Lacey each gave 23.
That's normal: 46.
But somehow there's another 21 –
3 copies, not just 2. We don't know why.
It's relatively common,
as defects go.'

'Could it happen twice?'
Gran said my father sat there like a post
cemented in the chair.

'Unlikely. There's no genetic history.
Your wife's still young.
Most families learn to cope.'

Are we most families?
Is my father's comfort
that at least I'm the second chance?

Sweet Mistake

Some nights I tuck my brother into bed.
His honey almond eyes gleam and dim.
His moon face shimmers in the dark.

I whisper, 'Now sleep tight' and then I think,
Rest easy, sweet mistake,
if that is what you are.

I turn but he sometimes grabs my hand,
holds it to his chest,
pretends to snore.

I feel the truth of his eager heart
that tries to love the world
without the strength to do it.

But it tries.

Lacey: The Good Mother

Philip's always been a good boy,
as good as he can be.
He tidies his room, clears his plate,
licks it when I make his favourite dish —
Worms Bolognaise. He's always been a good eater,
my healthy boy.

Once upon a time
Diana was my perfect little girl,
the gift from God I hoped for,
pink angel in my arms.
Robert snapped a hundred pictures then
to record this version of the future.

I bought Diana dresses, toys and books.
Baked her favourite, Chocolate Mouse,
used raisins for the eyes
and liquorice straps for tails.
Now no matter what I cook
she doesn't eat. Too busy with herself.

Too busy to make time for us.
God knows what she does with her time.
God knows what she'll do with her life.

Philip: I wish I could

I wish I could sleep tight, but no one's told me what that means. I asked Di once how to be tight and she just laughed and said I shouldn't worry. Worry keeps me up. So I pretend to snore to make her happy, but then she takes her hand away. I'm left alone. That's when they start to argue in my head. My nasty self, who makes me lose my temper, and the one Di loves.

I wish I could stop him bullying, turn off his voice and be the boss of me. He tells me that I want a snack. I push the pillow down around my ears. It doesn't help. I wish I could – so many things – sometimes it hurts.

Divine Ms D

I need to plan my life.
I won't leave things to chance.
Start with the basics – names –
and first research myself.

What have I got to work with?
My name, Diana, means *divine*.
So I've been right:
spirit always triumphs over flesh.

I'll push the truth of that.
So time to fall into the mythic past
to understand why things are as they are.
Why I am as I am.

But more, what I can be.

Lacey: Wrong

I still don't know what went wrong last year.
Robert almost washed his hands of her.
But after all, I said, she's our daughter.
Too clever for her good. The other day
she asked, 'What's the only word
that has 2 Ks, 2 Os, two Es?' I shook my head.

'Bookkeeper, Mother, just like you.'
'Accountant, dear,' I always have to correct.
Why does she do that? I work two days a week
to pay for Philip's helper.
Diana only takes him Saturdays,
and after all, he's her brother.

She could be a teacher,
was such an early reader,
sharing books with Philip:
The Magic Pudding, Alice's Adventures,
The Hobbit and his favourite, *Land of Oz.*
Those wonderlands were their second homes.

Sometimes I had to drag them back to ours,
to offer them something for their souls.
The saints are gateways to another world.
I told them tales of suffering and triumph.
'Our family has been tried as well,' I said.
'Let's hope we're not found wanting.'

Where has she gone?
It's dark.
Robert's in his office out the back.
Just Philip Bear and me in our cave,
warm from the crackling oven,
soothed by familiar smells.

I'll bake a fruit flan now
to complement the lamb,
recommended in that magazine.
There's time for that.
Diana isn't home.
Seems like there's always time.

Philip: The Last Tea Party

'At any rate, I'll never go there again!' said Alice as she picked her
way through the wood. 'It's the stupidest tea party I ever was at
in all my life!'
Alice in Wonderland

I always liked Alice. Tonight I tell Di I remember why because it's been
a bad day. I lost my temper twice. Alice "says to herself" like me. That's
how she figures things out. The "Drink me" bottle isn't marked poison
so she knows it's all right. She learns which side of the mushroom to
eat to grow and shrink. She has wonderful adventures by herself. "You
loved food more than adventure," Di says. And we laugh.

Once when I was small, Di gave me a tea party. After school Mum
let us move a table under the trees. This was a party just for us. While I
set out the cups and plates, Di went to the shop. She bought lamingtons
and jam tarts. Then we made Vegemite sandwiches and cut them into
triangles. We invited Humphrey Bear and Wombie, my old stuffed toys.

We drank tea with lots of sugar and ate and changed our seats. I
never saw Di laugh so much. Her eyes sparkled like stars.

'Twinkle, twinkle, little bat!

How I wonder what you're at!'

That was our theme song, Di said. We sang and giggled for ages. We
forgot who we were for real.

Then Dad came home and saw the mess, out in the yard where all
the neighbours could see. He said we were wasting time.

'Time to do what?' I asked.

'Your sister has homework to do.'

Di always had to be doing. Not me. We had to clean up quietly. We
crept around like mice. There were no mice at our party, not even a
sleepy dormouse. But we had to pretend. Di says to me now, 'We've
always been good at pretending.'

Recipe for the Good Life

I can't go home. Not yet.
Not close enough to dinner.
Philip and my mother
fill in time between each meal with snacks
and recipes that help eat up the day.
They don't cook tuck shop slop,
but play with Middle Eastern, Asian Fusion,
French, Indigenous. She drives me mad
with dumb clichés like this is 'Food for life,'
'Think of all the starving kids abroad,'
and worst, 'You know you are what you eat.'
I know she proves the last.
God creates all cuisines, great and small.
My mother's body shows she loves them all.

Robert: Master Builder

Another one of those days again –
it begins well enough. Philip is calm,
Lacey nags Diana out of bed.
Breakfast is cooked. I'm out the door on time.
There's order in my life.

10 am: My phone squirms on my belt.
It's Lacey. A minor irritation with a door.
Philip's banged it off one hinge.
I scratch and soothe. He doesn't know his strength.
I'll fix it when I'm home.

By six I'm back. Dinner smells great –
my favourite, saltbush lamb.
I offer to take Philip off her hands
now that he's finished peeling the potatoes.
He can cook a bit, my son. That's one thing.

Together we fix the door.
We haven't done that before.
I grab my tools and show him how to find
the right screws, how to check the level
so the door hangs straight.

Then Philip hefts it up, holds it in place
just as the phone rings and Lacey calls.
'Put it down a minute. I'll be back,'
I tell him as he balances the weight.
I leave him studying the rough wood grain.

When I return he's gone.
Then I hear him by my iron shed.
He's pulled the warped door off its rusty hinges.
'I checked the level too. It wasn't even.
We need to fix this too,' Philip says.

He's pulled with force enough to crack the wood.
The door is stuffed. So yet another job.
And then I see he's got a fair-sized splinter.
Philip realises, starts to wail.
Lacey hears us yelling on the lawn.

She screeches too, swells the family chorus.
Diana turns up, takes one look
and vanishes as usual.
I'm the one who's left to make repairs.
This is a job I can't retire from.

Retreat

Safe in my room. The door is thick,
the manic noise below becomes a storm
I've learned how to let pass. I turn the lock –
my mind roams where it wants to go.
First I pick apart the day,
create new scripts to cancel out
things that I didn't have to say.
My stupid tongue needs a talking to.

Then untamed thoughts swirl through.
I focus on his eyes – a thundery blue
against his navy shirt today.
My chair feels warm and wet.
I long to listen only to my body
that sings its own sweet song.
The sticky bed wants to lay me down.
Concentrate, I whisper. Ban the present.

The past has lessons that I need to learn.

Myths and Legends

Gran heard that I was researching myths
and ordered me this illustrated book.
I find the Greeks and Aborigines
made a sanctuary of the heavens.
Take that ancient stage, the Milky Way,
where Seven Sisters — or the Pleiades —
pursued on earth because they're beautiful
still act out their story of escape.

Orion tracks them through the winter sky
in the north. They can't flee to the south
for here the Ya-Ya men hunt beauty too.
The only refuge is run fast and high.
Is this long ago or here and now,
that sky this sky no matter what the names?
The virgin truth is keep yourself intact.
I read and find the theme's always the same.

Pare down the stories and the songs repeat
mythic notes dreamt in another climate.
Look at our night sky for the translation.
Here too I see that the heart is safe
only when it's like those distant stars —
untouchable themselves and proudly frozen.

Robert: Even Keel

I've built this family up,
given everything I have.
All I ask is some cooperation.
Diana does the minimal amount.
At least she sweet-talks Philip,
seems to really love him.
I don't know how – God knows I've tried.
Sometimes I wish...

She's the one with talent – read at four,
at ten played with words instead of Lego.
At fourteen she won a swag of prizes.
I told her then, 'You could be anything.
I would have been an architect,
but someone had to go and earn a living.
The farm would never be enough, Pop said.
And anyway, my brain is practical.'

Soon after, I don't know.
She shrank into herself. And stayed.
Lacey should have coaxed her out.
Her job's the family and I run the business.
Lacey tries. She cooks us gourmet meals,
lets Philip help her when he can,
so why is peace so hard to build?
We face the same old hassles every day.

Thank God I lined the new shed,
at least I have a space to work and think –
alone in peace – if there's a God to thank –
not the one Lacey's found of late.
Her charismatic mob's not rational.
Dear God, if you are real, please answer this:
am I the only one in this family,
who just wants life on an even keel?

My Mother's *Book of Saints*

That was my bedtime reading.
The only time we ever snuggled up
was for this weekly ritual.
Mother and daughter bonding
over saintly suffering,
the martyrs' blood washing away evil.

Communion through the stories of those lives –
chaste flesh transfigured into spirit
as the devil burnt them at the stake.
I watched my mother's lips. Would they tremble?
But she sat contented as an angel
when she read about the Roman Circus.

The naked faithful dragged and whipped,
mauled in the arena by wild beasts.
How could they call them Games
when no one ever fought back?

'That was the point,' my mother said –
That's what made a Passion,
a passive suffering that led to glory.
I held my breath, waiting for the worst.
When gladiators slit the martyrs' throats
I felt a blade singing in my heart.

History told me women suffered best,
always spared for the grand finale.
Yet this was how they won the game:
stripped and shamed yet powerful
by being what they were:
their own true selves exceptional in pain.

At night in bed I prayed:
all honour to the virgins
cool in the face of flames;
the wives who left their husbands
to battle with the beasts,
fulfilled in heaven by a godly groom.

Could I be that brave? Could I be worthy?
I felt their white-hot meaning in my bones:
'I am what choice has made me,'
every death proclaimed.

Lacey: The Gospel According to Lacey

God loves us all:
the martyr and the sinner,
the clever and the simple –
that's what I must believe.

I've opened up my heart to every creed
since God creates them all.
But this new church has made me realise
what hunger is.

I do feel born again,
nourished now by a greater family.
I let his Spirit fill me,
and testify that I've had my ordeals.

Diana has none. Always shuts us out.
I tell her I don't need another test.
God's done his best.
One Philip is enough.

She sees her father work without a break.
He sacrifices for our family's dreams.
We have a house, two cars, good food,
money in the bank – a life.

He only wants for her
to have some dreams,
to be as perfect as she can for us,
to learn not to be selfish.

Please, God, don't make me plead,
at least to her.
Help Diana be the daughter
that we need.

Namesake

1   Invocation

Lady of Wild Things, Apollo's twin,
unspoilt maiden goddess of the moon,
Mistress of Crossways, draped in black:
Artemis, Selene, Hecate, Diana.
Chased into life on a peak in Delos,
hunter-in-chief to the wayward gods.

Help me. Keep me faithful to my quest.

Watchful protector of the young
and all those who give them life,
pure guardian of birth, intact yourself,
you do not judge those who fall from grace.
Your silver arrows never miss their mark
but free your sisters into painless death.

Help me. Keep me faithful to my quest.

Diana, lover of woods and beasts,
above all, the deer to you is sacred —
with its graceful spring — and the evergreen cypress.
By day, slender as your arrows,
by night you swell, filling up the sky,
absorb the stars and give birth to chaste light.

Help me. Keep me constant in my quest.

2 Baptism

What did Diana, chaste hunter,
the sun's twin, love best?
Hounds, woods, herself?
Chase me for the answer.

I'm on her trail, hunting alter egos.
She won't escape, my namesake.
Scraps of myth, legendary lies,
tales of haughty heroes.
I century-hop, follow every scent.

Moon goddess, she maddened poets,
tantalising them in all her forms:
a slim rip in the dark, bleeding light;
a crescent hip draped in velvet,
a silver disc no male could spend.

Queen of Witches, Mistress of Magic,
Celtic mother, caster of charms,
prayed to by healing-women,
not so wise —
how many went up in flames?

When I was born Diana was a princess,
an English myth my mother loved.
But hunters know the fate of prey.
Stalked, snapped at, caught on film,
finally bailed up, dispatched.

I understand those royal secrets now.
How she purged herself
of everything that weighed her down —
family and sex — but she lost faith
in the one true path.

The lone girl pleasing no one
but her own cool self –
that's my namesake's meaning.
I snap my photos, film what's real,
document this shrinking life.

Subtract parents,
and brother fat with love.
Let my heart race on,
thrill at the chase:
untouched Diana's stern ideal.

Now pen my epithet
(I'm Libra, after all) –
Diana of the Scales
who hates the verb *to be*.
Listen. This is no passive voice.

I claim this name. This me.

An Odd Time of Year

'Gran's coming down to stay,' my mum says.

Philip starts to plan what they'll cook.
My dad stops mid-sip, his teacup poised
as if he's waiting for the camera's click.
I'd title this 'A man caught unawares.'

'An odd time of the year for her,' he says.
'Christmas is long gone.'

'She has some errands that she has to run.
She said she won't stay long.
There's hardly any shops in the Flinders.
I wonder she doesn't drive down more.'

'Mother's never worried about shopping.'

'Too much else deserves the energy.
Worry about only things that matter.
I'm quoting her,' I say.

But can I remember what they were,
those things that mattered to me as a girl?
Did anything make me weak with wanting?

Flinders Ranges

Astral Bodies

Driving north I entered another world,
Gran's "patch of paradise" she called it,
bordered by a saddle of bay mountains.
Her Handyman's Delight on an acre block
was nearly done when Pop retired from life.
She eased into a rocking chair and age,
alone and loving it. She had her books
and me to earbash when she got the chance.

My parents laid down rules – granny winked –
they drove away. And I was free to do
or be whatever, as long as I didn't maim
myself, harass the chooks, poison the dog
or burn the bush. No way, I thought.
This was my Promised Land, not the one
Mum sang about in church. This was heaven.
The first days there I mostly watched:

biting bull-ants swarming out of holes;
geckos pretending to be leaves
plastered on the cottage walls;
white cockatoos bursting from the gums
like hungry kids at recess. Then with Gran
I studied warblish – magpie language –
and coached the kangaroo Olympic team
hurdling through the paddocks.

On chilly nights we'd rock back to the past
scrunched in her rocking chair as we read
whatever took her fancy. Her head was crammed
with bits and pieces like a dress-up box.
She'd tell of Tiddalick, the greedy frog,

that drank the Flood. The Ugly Duckling,
'Like me with my best mate at our first dance.
We liked dogs more than we liked boys.'

'You know why women feel so much?' she asked.
'Que Sabe, The One Who Knows,
created us from wrinkles on her soles.
We've got no choice. We're tender and we're tough.'
At night we'd stare, stiff-necked, at the stars,
our dream map, story backdrop,
riding point-to-point across the heavens
chasing constellations.

We liked Centaurus best – the Centaur –
pawing stardust near the Southern Cross.
'In my book what needs to be reined in
comes from man, not horse. The horse part's natural.'
Well, I knew in my bones about that Centaur,
how he hated being stabled in a corner
of that infinite black pasture.
I knew about straining at the bit.

Later I'd drift asleep until I heard
his angry snort. Swept up on the wind
from his swishing tail, I'd untie his lead.
He'd toss me on his back and we'd escape,
galloping out of our proper forms
into a truer astral shape. No longer
animal or human, male or female,
forever shifting vivid points of light.

Flinders Ranges

Wolf Wind

In the belly of night at Gran's
I'd toss in the high brass bed where she was born.
After Pop died she chose a single cot.
'One body wide and a bit,' she said.
'I like to feel my boundaries.'
'Isn't it narrow?' I asked.
'Like the right road when you know where it leads.'

But I loved that mattress sprawl springy as her hips.
I'd do forward rolls into a pillow nest.
Make a wombat den. Crawl under the sheets.
Cool my toes on the tall brass posts.
Sleep any which way I chose. I was alone.
The rest of my family stayed in town.

On windy summer nights
when the house creaked like old leather,
I'd hunker down under the quilt,
only my hot dry nose poked out,
a sick puppy sniffing danger.

And then I'd hear them, keening on the wind,
impossible wolves I'd seen in books
prowling our feverish north.
One swollen with young,
all ragged and thirsty,
padding over the roof, howling for rain.

It was worst when the thunder stopped.
I'd kneel at the window, exhausted with sweat,
and see above only a dim graveyard,
the wolves now dead, a shadowy huddle,

already dissolving in some god's hot breath,
the odd bone gleaming.

Sometimes, slashed by lightning,
the wolves lingered in pain, moaning all night,
bleeding out at dawn.
Then I'd slip back beneath the quilt,
tracking whatever myths we needed
to make it rain.

Flinders Ranges

First Love

i Changeling

I was born into the wrong pack,
or maybe fairies migrated with Pop
when he took the ship from England.
Maybe, delirious in the heat,
they confused their magic,
left a weakling daughter to his son.
Or maybe they stole just the right seed
of an idea from my mother's stock –
a sturdy girl with legs
made to swing over a horse.

But as a flabby kid, I was useless.
Only at Gran's I had the chance to learn
how to be at home in my own skin.
Then one summer when I was thirteen
a family appeared on the neighbouring farm.
'Hobbyists,' Gran said, 'not serious.
But nice. They sold their shop in town.'
One child – Clara – the type I should have been.
Older than me, but crazed with loneliness,
any kid would do as her apprentice.

For three whole weeks she had me to herself.
We fed her cheeky bantams,
skinned our knees climbing stunted wattles,
chain-sneezed together, collapsed with laughter
watching piglets, farty little beach balls,
latching onto teats as long as fingers.

Then there were the horses.
I went wild with love and fear.
First she dinked me on her ancient pony –
twelve hands three – back like a slippery dip.
Next she showed her champions.
I stood in awe as she worked them both:
walk, trot, change diagonal,
watch that lateral movement. But the canter –
when they rocked together,
muscles quivering in harmony,
the dust rolled up in sympathetic clouds –
the mists of time – and she became a Centaur,
girl and animal fused,
feeling what she could be in her bones.

ii First Flight

Horses perch on their toes – their hooves –
always ready to flee. Tasty prey,
a meal for wolves, any sharp-toothed predator
that harried their ancestors
still hunts them in their genes.

Even with bellies full on a grassy plain,
they're ready to take off and at the gallop
hang suspended for an instant,
four feet in the air.

I plucked titbits like that from books,
hungry for whatever made me worthy.

One night Clara called late.
'Turn up at 5 am.
Time for your first ride out before it's hot.'
I dressed in jeans, biked over.
She'd saddled up already before dawn.

I'd trotted round on Sam, the quarter horse,
the smaller of her two,
and sat a lazy canter.
Goblin Mist, the thoroughbred,
her great grey hope, was only for herself.

We walked them out into a world
that dark had gentled, stroking every outline.
The horses, fresh but easy,
stretched their noses down,
nuzzling at the green fuzz left by sheep.

Air was flavoured with a hint of wattle.
Cockatoos rustled from the gums
to peck at bits of chaff.
The flies were dopey,
no anxious whirring yet to cut the quiet.

When we reached a bend in the path
Clara said, 'Shorten your reins'
and suddenly fired ahead
as if a hungry beast were on her tail.

Sam knew what that meant
and leapt, a heartbeat behind,
like a second rifle shot.
Together, we sliced through wind and dust

but Clara dashed ahead,
flattening on her horse's neck
till once again she and he were one.
Then 'Go' reared in my brain.

I urged Sam on, embracing him,
fingers in his mane, and laughed.
'Okay?' Clara shouted back.
My blood so loud she must have heard.

Stretching out, the two of us,
this natural way of being *we*,
balanced on his neck so he could fly –
that was it – this being *we* –

a streamlined creature we became.
We, I felt, *we*, I breathed,
losing all control and zooming forward
we, two but one, *we* flew as one

all four feet in the air,
racing Clara for no prize but speed
till the world blurred but *we* were clear –
galloping into being here.

Now I knew how I could survive.
We we we we drumming out the infinite,
each perfect second of it.
I was terrified alive.

iii Drought

I was in love with Clara and her horses.
I knew I could weather drugged autumn days,
my brain dusty as our city garden,
if time could gallop half as fast as Sam.

Winter swept in with lukewarm rain
but not enough to fill the reservoirs.
Once the concrete birdbath froze,
its mirror glazed over like my eyes.

I lived only for the next visit,
swallowed down the pain of separation
till midyear break and my resurrection
as a daggy, horse-mad country girl.

Then another wait until hot winds
blew me north again. Their feverish tongues
licking off the land until each dam
shrunk into the sockets of a skull.

Finally last term's holidays – salvation.
Gran's yard had baked into toughened glass
like dirty windows in abandoned houses.
She had bad news, knew what it meant for me.

'Running a small farm with only one dam,
hard in a dry season. A corporation
gobbling little ones up. Not many buyers
otherwise. Best to get out when you can.
They've enough for another shop, a house behind.
And they'll agist the horses somewhere near.'

Clara and her family lasted two years.

Family Dinner

Gran arrives today.
I haven't seen her in six months.
My mother says she's in the big smoke,
for a doctor's visit and some shopping.
The drive from up north takes it out of her.
My father says she has no trouble coping.

At dinner my mum's Hallelujah patter
makes her wink at me. I pass the sauce –
sweet and sour – for the duck,
just manage not to laugh.
'Good to see you in a pleasant mood –
for once,' Mum says.

'Down to me,' Gran quips.
'Everyone agrees I'm laughable.'

'Well, you should drop in more.'
My father nods at her.

'Unless I learn to parachute
"dropping in" doesn't quite describe
a five-hour drive on country roads.

Though out of practice,
Dad has to grin.

'You lot can drive due north,'
Gran tosses this suggestion up
and waits for an answer to float down.

She glances at me then.
'When's the last time that you came?'
Her eyes are foggy blue,
a winter sky threatening rain.

My father scrapes his chair.
'The business doesn't run itself
and Diana has to finish school.
It's taken long enough.'
His mouth can't help but twitch.
'Then a full-time job is on the cards.
She's got lots on her plate.'

Gran sniffs and lifts one brow.
'And what plate would that be?'
She points at mine.

'Diana only picks,' my mother says.
'Eats like a bird.
Girls her age do.'

'When I was a girl,' Gran begins,
'centuries ago,
we knew the value of a good meal.
Are girls so different now?'

'Yes, Mother, you've told us more than once,
your life was hard.'
My father shakes his head.

'That's why I want to help.
Come stay awhile.'

Philip almost spills his juice.
'I want to go to Gran's. Can we?'

My father puts his glass firmly down.
'Lacey couldn't cope alone.
And I can't take the time to drive that far.'

Gran sighs and crosses knife and fork.
'She wouldn't be alone. I'd be there, too.'

She fixes now on my mother.
'Come on, let down your hair.'

'Absolutely not,' Dad says.
'Be realistic, Mum.'

'Realistic?' Gran's voice grates
as if she's braked on gravel.
'Look around...'

Philip's stomach makes the only sound.

Pale Faces

After dishes, Gran takes me aside.
'What's up, sweet pea? Not sick? You hardly ate.'

'Of course I did,' I counter.

'A smear of veg, a scrap of meat
that wouldn't bait a mousetrap.'
She strokes my cheek. 'You're very pale, Diana.'

'And so are you.'
Suddenly I see she really is.
Her skin's a weathered marble,
like statues in my book of myths.
'Are you OK?' I ask.
'You're here to see a doctor, aren't you?'

'Don't worry. I'll go on forever —
in one form or another.'
She squeezes me and feels my ribs.
'You're far too thin, my girl.
You'll disappear and who knows if they'll notice.'

I hug her back and think,
she's thinner too.

'Come up to visit, please? Next holidays.
I know there aren't horses . . .'

'I was over all that years ago.'

'Then humour me in my old age,' she chuckles.
'I'd like to think sometimes I had a family.'

Gran nods off before the TV.
My mother shakes her so she'll go to bed.

'Trip's worn me out. I'm boring, I know.'
She kisses us and shuffles up the stairs.
I wait half an hour and then follow.

Good. Her light is off. I hear her snore.
I grab my robe, slip to the bathroom,
turn the shower on full bore.
Then notice a familiar smell.
Has she been sick? I can't waste time.
Philip's program's almost done.
He'll be up soon. I kneel. The tiles are cold,
perfect for my cleansing ritual.

Myth Mother

That's the way I always think of Gran.
She told me ancient stories,
taught stargazing, astral travelling.
It's why I dream myself into the heavens.

I could transform into anything
pure enough to reach that pure black space
if I was good, sacrificed enough
to rearrange the stars into my story.

Now that she is leaving,
my insides feel like a nightmare sky
emptied of its lights,
and hungry for her brand of honesty,

the kind that never offers gift-wrapped words,
but the plain unribboned truth.
That's what I've always loved about my gran.
That's what my father hates.

Philip: Care Bear

Sit here, Care Bear, we need to talk just like Mum and Dad sit down when I've been bad. So look at me when I talk to you. I'm feeling sad.

I haven't talked much to you this month. I can be boss of my mouth. But now I need your ears again. You were Di's but now you're mine, so listen.

I feel bad because I broke a rule. Or I think I did. I'm not supposed to come into Di's room unless she says. But all I did was peek. I heard her voice.

And there was a crack that fit my eye. I saw Di talking to her mirror just like I talk to you.

This is what she said. 'Chocolate freak. Butter bum – fat face, fat thighs, fat tits.' And then she pinched herself – hard – whispering, 'You deserve to starve.' She shouldn't hurt herself. That's what she made me promise when I'm angry.

'My Hulk' Di always calls me – good to squeeze. I'm her block of chocolate, family size. That's what she says. And everyone loves chocolate.

So how can she be fat when I'm the block? And doesn't everyone really love chocolate?

Lesson on Bones

Big-boned, raw-boned, fine-boned, bird-boned —
human frames trap us in the picture
of our type. Our shape. Our home.
Our comfy skeleton. Our 206-room house.
Small, medium, large: what choice do we have?
None. The genetic menu's fixed.

What kind of house do I want to be?
One blessed by a svelte hearth sprite
with ethereal pedigree.
A classically proportioned temple,
fashioned from mist, the glint of marble,
the goddess's breath.

Done growing, I can sketch my body plan.
The skeleton: twenty percent adult weight —
negotiable the rest.
Time to trim the excess. I admire
bones too much to tamper with perfection.
The Master Builder cuts no corners.

Hear that, Father?

What lesson have I learned from all of this?
Why not unveil the work of art I am?
Peel off the flesh, reveal the spine of truth.
These bones began before my birth,
will outlast death. My immortal rulers,
they help me to measure up.

Revelations

1 Songs of Praise

'Who wants to testify?'
My mother loves pop hymns,
singing while she cooks.

Father Sceptic asks how long to dinner,
not salvation.
It's late tonight, past seven –
his inner clock's ticked off.

Mother, born again,
sings another phrase and points her spoon:
'Patience is a virtue. Soon.'
She praises Jesus King.

Dad stops and turns.
'I'll be out back,' he says.
'Now here's a revelation for you, Lacey.
You might be saved, but you still can't sing.'

2 Paradise Gained

The charismatic music filters in.
As I doze in a lounge chair God appears,
granting me a technicolour vision –
the real thing, no phony Wizard here.
In Lacey's heaven Philip will be born
a second time with all his cells in order.
She is the perfect Mother of the Year
and Diana finally is the perfect daughter.
With tears, Robert washes Lacey's feet
and joins the choir to pay off his sins.
Then as a family they sit down to eat;

everyone in Paradise stays thin.
The blessed chorus line comes with the sweets:
a thousand angels dancing on a pin.

Temptation

There he is, that boy from class.
Don't stare. Sip your latte.
This café's packed. He won't notice me.

The way he moves reminds me of that colt
by grandma's place nearly ten years back —
free and easy. What a leggy beauty,

and so is Conor striding to the bar.
Look at those glossy girls
shoving to make space for him —

a lean male with tangled chestnut hair.
Wait till they hear his voice,
its welcome rhythm and swing.

Makes me think of Irish pubs in town
with jigs and reels spilling out the door,
inviting anyone in.

Makes me think as well there's more to him
than meets the eye. Sometimes the eye's enough.
I envy that he seems so much himself.

Their order comes. The girls have to give way.
Now Conor has his meal he needs a seat,
scans the room. Our eyes lock for an instant.

I jump, caught out, retreat to reading. What?
Black figures prance before me on the page,
then freeze when the other seat scrapes out.

'Mind if I sit?'
'Fine. It's free.'
He slides his crowded tray over to mine.

The silky smell of melted mozzarella,
tomatoes, garlic, basil,
makes my nostrils flare.

Some temptations are easy to resist.
I choose another, sitting opposite,
look up and smile.

Conor: First Lunch

Can't keep my bloody mouth shut. She sits there, hardly says a word, watching me talk myself into a corner. If I bolt she'll really think I'm an idiot. Mother always said I ran like a tap as a lad and only Father's boot would turn me off.

Is she judging me or what? I can't tell and if I stare that'll do for me. But she smiled when I sat down. That's what I noticed first about her in class, though she's stingy with it. Not a flashy smile, all sunshine and such, but surprising. More moonlight than glare. I make her grin when I tell about our blue heeler who walked sideways on a fence to grab his ball out of a tree.

She's typical Libra, she says. Wonder what that means. She tells me I'm a Taurus, atypical, too tall. But a bull, tied to home. Too right, but I'm far from it.

'Who did I come with?' she asks. Just my father and me. Mother died five years back. Father's still not over it. Nor am I, but I don't tell her that. Sounds soft and I'm not sure what kind of lads she's used to here. She'd have plenty.

So I tell her about the horses, the racing part. Some girls think 'it's all so exciting,' then lose interest. They don't want to know about the blasted paddocks and the grit that eats its way into your soul or your muscles aching after you've worked six horses, made up the feeds, mucked out the stalls, hauled down the hay bales, as if you'd galloped a mile yourself.

She listens, though, and asks questions. Keeps asking. We talk long after we've finished lunch. Or I have. She says she ate a big breakfast. Doesn't look it. She'd blow away in a stiff wind.

Maybe lunch tomorrow, I ask? She nods, just. Those blue-green eyes don't show much – glowing cat's eyes, taking it all in. I'd like to make her purr all right.

Irish Dreamer

Lunch tomorrow, same café.
Idiot! Why didn't I say coffee?
Those eyes, I guess –

shocking blue,
high-noon summer eyes.
This charming Irish lad, I suspect,

is steely underneath.
His life sounds anything but lyrical
if you listen for the silences between

the lilting words. He spins a lovely yarn
about their great adventure – 'me and Father' –
(the mother dead) coming to Australia

to mend their fortunes, break the family cycle.
I think I've seen this tale before –
poor migrant makes good in the promised land.

I only nod and smile.
He reads my face and laughs.
'The truth? We weren't hard up.

Just doomed to be middling middle-class.
We've been so close.'
'To what?' I ask.

'Success. That win to set us up for life –
my father's words.
I've learned to take what comes.'

His dad's the dreamer. Conor's got his feet
cemented in the ground.
'Had to,' he says. 'I'll never make a jockey.

I had my dreams of Grand National glory
since I was nine. But then at seventeen
I grew to five foot ten – in one year.

Felt worse than if I'd fallen in a race.
Broken bones can heal but I don't know
how you can make them shrink. I guess I'm stuck

the way I am.' He doesn't see me now.
He's somewhere inside, feeling that black dog
pawing at his heart. Then he snaps back.

'And the way I am is six foot one.'
 'Too big for your own boots then,' I say.
'So what's the plan now?'

'Train. The family business.
I've got a colt,' he begins and stops.
'But that's another story. I've got lots.'

'I bet you have,' I laugh.
He checks his watch. 'Sweet Jesus.
Let's walk,' he says. 'We're late.'

He guides me up and through the door
into the humid afternoon.
Our shoulders touch and stick.

'Then why school?' I ask as we trot off.
'My fallback plan. Some kind of a degree
in agriculture, animal husbandry.'

We're nearly at the gates. I slow and turn.
'Would you go home?
Ireland I mean.'

'Father wouldn't. I'd hate to leave him here,'
Conor shades his eyes.
'Mother's there for him.

He'd miss her something fierce.'
His voice sounds anything but.
And you as well, I think.

Conor: Climate Change

What I miss most is green. The misty morning grass that crushed sweet under the horses' hooves as I led them out from the field. And my father's fields fringed by sycamores, larches and oaks, with their leaves flapping in a brisk wind making the horses skittish. The leaves shiny like cooking apples. Typical of my family's luck. We sold up just before the housing boom reached us and money started flowing into our county from Dublin.

Our land bordered a lake there. I remember how the swans scattered in the dawn when I hauled the stroppy geldings past. Horses always mean early starts. We needed to work them before we headed for the jobs that gave us cash so we could keep the gallopers going. We left our three acres in early April when the days stretched out towards twelve at midsummer night. Still a lick of cold in the air. It was cobweb light again by four.

It's crazy here. So much is reversed. Native swans are black as my dress boots, not a proper white like ours. Green's a winter colour mostly. I'm still not used to summer. I sneeze every time that bloody north wind gusts and the heat squeezes me so I drip like a dishcloth. Coated with sunblock, I think we're ready for frying. The fields – paddocks they call them here – toast under the sun as if they had given up hope. I know they're just playing dead now, biding their time until the season breaks in April. If it breaks at all. But even beaten down this is my father's land – fifteen acres, more than he could afford in Ireland.

A few weeks ago we had a grand gift – a shower in a dry month. It dusted the paddocks with green. Kikuyu grass is mostly what we've got. At first we didn't know how lucky we were. It's as stubborn as Father and grasping as any weed. That old grey mare we bought to teach the colt some manners, she nibbles the shoots as soon as they appear and already she's put on weight.

I don't go to Church anymore, not since Mother died, but when the evening sea breeze rolls in, it's like I've been to confession again and the priest's granted me absolution. If the tide goes out at dusk and it's cool, we can exercise the horses on the beach.

Dawn's my favourite time now, even if I've had a late night at the pub. There's a busy kind of quiet. Cockatoos strip the acacias and crackle over the seedpods that litter the grass. Galahs peck at leavings in the feed bins. The clockwork magpies snatch at dung beetles. Whatever the hot day holds for me hasn't begun to pulse in my temples.

That's when I saddle up Quinn, the sherry-bay colt with the white blaze, and take him to the beach. That's where I get to know what he's made of. The shore's wide and flat, swept clean by receding waves. It unfurls like a cat's tail from the jetty towards the ridge and a horse can stretch its full length, nose reaching into the breeze. As I crouch over Quinn's neck, we flatten out in a line that I like to think might never end. Tears leak from my eyes, my cheeks tighten as if I've got a bit in my mouth too, and someone's hauling me back. But I run on. That's why living here's worth it.

Lunch Again

Conor wonders I'm not turning green,
thinks I'm nine-tenths rabbit.
Salad's all I eat.

For now I'll pay the price
for this type of temptation.
I feel I've almost woken

after years of sleep.
He's opened the glass coffin
but hasn't kissed me yet.

He knows the way he stares at me
whets our appetites for something more.
My insides stir when our fingers brush

as he flips through the menu to desserts.
Luscious words alone could weigh me down:
cocoa fantasy, Kahlua cream.

His voice, too, a dangerous invitation.
I pack up and choose escape
into a surprising summer rain

that soaks us through, revealing what we are.
We can't help but look. I touch his throat –
the fair skin's slick as stone.

Suddenly I ask,
'What do you miss the most?'
He doesn't hesitate. 'Green.'

Tales of Gods and Heroes

At the State Library

I'm here to study myths and not to dream
of Conor's knowing hands that stroke my hair,
my face, my perfect self, until it seems
there never was another. But the glare
of soaring glass melts my confidence,
this cocksure entrance that now shadows me.

I have some faith that myths can still make sense —
they last because they have that clarity
of knowing who we are. Does Conor know?
I reach to touch the fine hairs on his chest —
and snap myself awake. I need to show
some self-control, my dad would say. A test
of character. So back to work. My choice
to excavate the past and not the present,
to let myself imagine how each voice
betrays its soul. I feel so adolescent
compared to what I read. A paperback
whose tales seem too familiar. Why? They're soaps.
In this yellowing fifties' artefact
uncensored antique dramas fuelled by hope.

And then there are the long quests fired by lust
and greed, soaked in blood, most anything
for spice. Like a dismembering of trust
and bodies. Bestiality is king —
the king of gods, Zeus, often changes shape —
a swan or bull, whatever helps to charm
an unsuspecting virgin who learns rape
has consequences far beyond the harm
it does to her. The world forgets her pain,
remembers most the demigods she bears —

children in whom beauty and chaos reign.
Helen of Troy for one. I try to care
about them, but I can't. I start to hate
the passiveness of victims, all those women
who endure the petty whims of Fate.
They are done to without having done.

One thing I know: I want to know I've done.

Guilt

'I think you might do something better with the time,' she
said, 'than wasting it in asking riddles that have no answers.'
   'If you knew Time as well as I do,' said the Hatter, 'you
wouldn't talk about wasting it. It's him.'
Alice in Wonderland

I kiss his cheek, apologise
for leaving him alone so much.
'I understand,' he says,
'you can't waste time with me.'

'Let's not blame time,' I answer.
He waits for me to name the guilty party.
'I've murdered him more than once.'
We cackle at old jokes.

I promise that we'll read as in the past.
Sometimes I think the past's a trap –
our crazy games, our comfort reads
when we would squeeze together on the bed.

But what a sweet escape.
I owe my brother that.
If I repay the debt
maybe Time will find the time
to forgive me, too.

Time for Bed

The pillow changes shape beneath my head.
I close my eyes,
picture a riverbank where a small girl waits
for something good to happen.

That's me, plump and twitchy –
not a long-haired Alice lazing through golden days,
but a filly who bolts at sudden noise,
wide eyes taking life in.

And Alice's adventures
were only dreams.
She woke to a real illusion –
an innocent child.

There are no wonderlands or emerald cities.
Dorothy's fantasies were never true.
Back in Kansas, life moved on without her.
Uncle Henry rebuilt the house.

Love or not, why wouldn't you long to leave
that sterile place for a land where beauty and terror
made your heart beat faster, and you fit in
because people there were stranger than you?

At home we had our own tornadoes –
parents slamming doors, weeping, shouting.
Philip and I built a pillow shelter,
hoping that would help us weather the storm.

Time's kind to exhausted children.
He covered us with sleep, froze the moon,
let her melt across the sky,
then kept watch till dawn.

The miracle was everything slowed down.
Light crept through the window,
politely touched my face.
The day seemed possible again.

Library: Passion and Ideals

Conor and I stay after class.
I said I'd help him with the play he chose
for independent study.
We find a desk hidden in the stacks.

Our knees graze under the desk.
He leans and whispers so that I can hear.
My senses spark:
apples and honey scent his hair.

'You only chose *Equus* for the title.'
'Horses are what I know about,' he says.
'That doesn't mean it's easy,' I point out.
'Why not look at the boy's ideals?'

'Ideals?' he snorts. 'The boy
sacrifices to his weird abstraction,
a God-horse mixed with sex.
But animals suffer here and now.'

Conor sounds annoyed.
His hair swings in his face.
My heart swings in my chest,
but I pull back – defend the play, the boy.

'I know it's just a metaphor of sorts,'
Conor huffs, 'but look where blind devotion leads.
OK, Shaffer wants us to admire
that someone in the play at least feels passion...'

'Shaffer's made you passionate as well.'
Conor laughs. 'I do fine on my own.
And when it comes to horses,
I feel their fear and pain.

The lad blinds them when he thinks he's failed.
He thinks too much. The mind can be a trap –
brooding warps and shrinks.
You squirm inside and suddenly can't move.'

Conor holds his breath. Then he turns.
Looks into my soul.
'Sometimes you can stretch between the bars.'
He does and strokes my hand.

Fallback

As we left Conor asked, 'What's your plan?'

'Plan A or Plan B?' I returned.

'No word games now,' he said. 'You always win.
Plan A and B and any fallback schemes.'
His X-ray eyes swept me up and down.
'It's time for truth. What do you want to be?'

I felt my bones glow
and almost said, 'Perfect,'
but couldn't bring myself. It sounded slim.

I shrugged and grabbed his arm.
I don't think in years like him.
He's always moving towards, not away.
He moved me towards the trees near the bus,
a singed patch now in shadow.
We slipped between thick-waisted gums,
the anxious leaves seemed rattled.
I almost ran. Almost. The wind soothed.

My back found something firm and rough.
We kissed – just.
His hand cupped my head and pulled me close.
It was dusk. Were we drunk?
We swayed and almost fell.
I tangled his mane of hair,
he lost his fingers in mine.
We shivered and stroked.

His tongue traced my neck.
Our mouths were dusky and deep,
night rolling us up
and tucking us in.

Did this feel like dying?
The leaves fell silent.

Then we heard the bus hum,
calling us back to now.
We stumbled from the trees,
trying to see in the glare.
Conor helped me on. In a blink
I was gone.

Gone. Gone.

The Scent of Memory

Twelve o'clock. The sky is pocked with stars.
Gauzy cloud bandages the moon.
She is pale and ill.
Does she feel betrayed?
Is she owed a sacrifice?
Could I sacrifice him?

Now I lay me down in my single bed
still wrapped in the day's heat.
The moon tries to spy into my business
but I shift out of her searchlight.
Are the old always jealous?
Grandma never pried.

What's that smell on my pillow,
new yet familiar?
I fall back into grandma's kitchen —
baked apples spice the air.
I cut earrings from the peels,
looped them through my hair.

Damp and sweet, finally I fall asleep,
his green scent flavouring my skin.

Conor: Driving Blind

Somehow we got to the bus. She vanished so fast I couldn't think of what to say. She's blindsided me and I feel as if I'm just waking up from a dream where I don't know where I am. My eyes are open but dazed by images born out of the dark and those blasted memories I can't keep from creeping in like rats in the feed bins.

The back of the bus blurs in the twilight. I can still feel her cheek rubbing mine like a cat marking her territory. I need to catch hold of the dream she is before I lose her. Something inside needs so much — it's like the hope I used to feel before a race when I'd gathered my reins, set my legs and the horse was ready to jump. Maybe she's more a dark star than a dream, drawing me in when I kiss her.

I somehow find my car through the evening haze. As I leave the city I speed to keep pace with my heart. I'd better watch those ruby cat's eyes marking the road. Her eyes aren't red, they flash blue-green. Her face pops up on the windscreen and blinds me, just like those brights when some driver zips past without dimming. I'd better look sharp, especially when I reach the road near the dam where roos gather. They've got no sense, and the headlights dazzle them. I turn on the radio, sing along with some dumb pop tune whether I know the words or not, then try out falsetto. Haven't done that for a while. It used to make Mother laugh till she'd cry. Father too. He didn't need to be full of whiskey to break up like that.

I haven't been really drunk in a while. Five years ago Father was for a week and then gave up the drink till we left Ireland. Now he only has so many glasses and stops, measuring out what's left of his life. But he still gets the shakes whenever we come to a blind corner. He remembers the wheels screeching like banshees, and lights in his head as if a hundred bulbs popped at once. Kids singing themselves home from the pub, having the time of their lives. They totalled Father's car, flipping it over, but not theirs. They limped away. Mother didn't. Maybe some of them are as immortal as they think. Some days when I remember what happened I'd like to go back to help them find out.

Suddenly I'm exhausted with too much feeling. I've just passed that wreck parked outside the garage near the dam. So I turn up the radio till my ears ring. Give myself a good talking to.

'Wake yourself, lad. You don't want to end up looking like a squeeze box.'

At least the moon's rising, a nice fat face in the sky smiling me home. Yes, this is home now. Day or night, I'm getting used to seeing in this light.

Hunted

Alone again, me and my books, my myths.
I can't concentrate with Conor here.
His scent's too strong,
that sweetness could be fatal.

Who's pursuing whom?
Who cast the spell
to make us circle like two dogs?

I close my eyes and drift into a dream
of what might be,
feel his tongue lick my mouth,
his teeth grab those stray hairs at my neck
and gently pull. His panting at my ear.
I toss my glossy head, arch my back.
We both growl. And come.
Part of me hates it all – being in heat.

Daphne Revisited

I read and write about her,
but I'm the one who worries I'm transformed.

Daphne, virgin huntress,
was daughter of a minor river god
who granted her a wish:
to keep herself aloof, intact and free,
as her model, chaste Diana, was.
Cynical Ovid tells the tale.
Apollo's pride and lust
make him wager Cupid.
Who's pursuing whom?
Here it's clear.

Ovid lets his Apollo wonder
what this lovely object of desire,
sweaty mistress of the woods,
would look like as willing wife
dressed in tasteful robes,
her tresses up and tamed.

Daphne flees, prays to her father-god,
another man, to help her keep her vow.
He grants the wish by metamorphosis,
so cancels out what made her what she was.

Her limbs grow numb, rooted in the earth.
The rich smell of decay floods the air.
She's paralysed as a laurel tree,
whose branches can never shrug off despair.

Runaway

I couldn't say no.
He's been asking me to visit
his wee bit of Ireland in the scrub,
to show off his horses, his windy beaches,
to get me alone again, I think, I hope.
Will he take me for a ride?
Part of me wants to run away.
Part of me just wants to run.

I've been pleading work and Philip as excuses.
'You want to pass and graduate?'
I asked, touching his cheek.
'That's no way to make me work,'
he laughed, squeezing my waist.
'You need some fun, to get away from home.'
If he really knew . . .

Mum seemed pleased and surprised I wanted time off.
I was surprised and pleased she let me have it.
Philip threw a fit.
He's used to Saturday outings in the park.
I promised tomorrow, hugged and soothed.

But when Conor arrived he hid.
I was sort of glad.
When I left I heard him arguing upstairs.
I hope Care Bear's on my side.

Poor Mum.
It's going to be one of those days.
Poor me.
When I get home, I'll pay.

Recipe for Success

'See that chestnut and the grey?
They're in top form.
And here's my little beauty, Quinn, the bay.'

I forgot how amazing horses are.
His flanks glow like amber,
a whisper of ribs beneath the skin.
His muscled haunches from the rear
look like a ripe apple
and promise turbo power.

I lift my hand to touch his face.
'Don't worry, he won't bite —
unless you deserve it,' Conor says.
Quinn's ears twitch, his coffee eyes
watch me closely.
He lets me stroke his creamy blaze
and rub his muzzle.
Its softness seems newborn.

'You've passed the test,' Conor laughs.
'Lucky for you. And me.'

'I can see why he's your prize.'

'Wait till you see him move.
Come on, before we ride
we'll mix the feeds for Father.
He's at the track today.
We'll both be late from town.
After all, I have to drop you home.'
His voice grows quiet. 'Unless you stay.'
I smile and shrug. 'I can't.'

We line six buckets up,

measure out chaff, maize, oats,
sunflower seeds and lupins.
Conor loads them in a wheelbarrow.
'Molasses, vinegar and oil
we mix in right at dinnertime.'

'We should be taking Chemistry,
or maybe Potions with this wizard's brew.'

'I hope it works its magic.
Too fat, a horse can't keep the pace.
Too thin, he can't perform.
Energy is the key. And proportion.'

'Does that mean how they look is how they run?'

'Not quite that easy,' Conor says,
wheeling the barrow to the stable.
'But if they're fit and feeling well,
they'll try their best.
That's the only recipe for success.
You don't just breed a winner.'

We unload the feeds near the stable.
Quinn whinnies, kicks his stall.
'He's feeling good all right,
he wants his dinner.'

'Work first, then eat.
That's the rule.
Come on, let's saddle up.'

Second Flight

When we reach the top of the track,
wind slaps us in the face –
me and the dozy mare I'm on.
Sandhills roll away on either side,
waves of scrub blanketing the coast.

Conor plucks white berries
from a prickly tea-green bush and hands me some.
'You wouldn't think they're sweet, growing here.'
He's right. Everything's thin, sparse,
but their roots must be strong.

Below, the beach spreads like an ochre road,
then disappears round a curve.
'Dead flat. Perfect.' Conor nods to me.
'Come on. You said you rode a bit. Let's see.'

We shuffle down through deep sand.
My mare trips, rights herself.
Young Quinn plunges ahead, stumbling too,
like Philip at ten, desperate to jump in the sea.

This sea's a fine silk shawl,
turquoise blue shot through with jade.
Hardly a ripple,
though small waves tease the shore.

We walk to the foamy edge.
The horses' hooves print the boggy sand.
Quinn snorts and prances sideways.
'He's keen to go. He knows the drill.'

Conor pats his lathered neck,
barely conceals his pride.
'Your old girl raced a while ago
and can't be bothered now.'

Misty snorts and pricks her ears at that.
And all I see ahead is space,
an open invitation.
Does she feel my fear, my hesitation?

Conor wheels Quinn back to where it's hard.
'Ready? Shorten your reins.
Quinn'll be off like Formula One.
Let Misty set her own pace.'

Conor smiles as if he's won the Cup.
He leans forward.
Quinn bolts from a walk,
flings his tail out, shoots ahead.

Misty jumps, charging in his wake.
I can't believe how fast she moves,
changing gears from three beats to two,
remembering what she was bred for.

I feel transparent, the wind whistling through.
We'll never catch Quinn, but I don't care.
I flatten into her line,
so we fly over the sand.

I forgot what it's like to forget,
to vanish and be filled with speed.
I cling to her neck,
at the still centre of her racing world.
I am no one

I am no one thing
but muscle and tears
sweat and breath

I could die this way.

I could live this way, too.

Conor: Beach Ride

Once we were on the road Diana spent most of the time watching the scenery roll past. I wanted to ask where her brother Philip had been, because I never saw him. She's told me a bit about Down Syndrome, and how she has to help because her mother can't always cope. When I was in the hall I heard voices upstairs, but Diana pulled me out the door without even a cuppa, saying we didn't have time to waste.

When we got home I gave her the grand tour on the little tractor before I showed her the horses. She seemed to light up then. And Quinn gave her the sniff of approval. She'd told me she could ride a bit, learned in the mid-north at a neighbour of her gran's. So I had planned a beach ride. Gave Diana the old mare, Quinn's paddock mate, who's only 15'2.

Maybe I was crazy to gallop. When I gave Diana a leg-up on Misty, I wondered for a minute if she'd be all right, because she weighs next to nothing. She'd only have balance and nerve for controls. Still, when we rode out she clicked straight off with Misty. Looked like she'd been riding for years.

Quinn loves the beach and as soon as we feel that salt breeze he always struts down the sandhills. Last night's April rain had swept away the seaweed. The waves rippled like a green cloak, the sky was watercolour blue, it was the kind of day that makes me forget I was ever born anywhere else.

When we hit the flat, I let Quinn have his head and did he run! When I turned to check, there was Diana not far back, flattened down on Misty like a grey jetstream. I didn't think that old mare could still move that fast. We galloped the full length of the beach till we reached the curve of the bay and I pulled Quinn up.

Diana grinned and her blue-green eyes were glinting like the sea. We didn't say a word, just sat huffing with the horses as we looked out to the horizon. All of us, me and Diana and Quinn and Misty, just glad to be alive in this moment, in this place.

Speeding

I'm speeding even though I'm standing still.
Misty is more relaxed than me.
Nervy Quinn paws the dirt but settles
once Conor ties him up next to the mare.
No words are needed in this busy silence.
We undo saddles, hose off sweaty skin,
walk the horses round until they're cool.
They're satisfied now that they've had their run,
their taste of freedom. Hay is what they're after
and sweet surprises mixed into their feed.

Conor's after something else, I think.
Even though we move in separate circles
around our munching horses, cutting apples,
tidying their gear, sweeping out stalls,
I catch his eyes, uncompromising blue,
tracking me everywhere I work.
Quinn's reassured by Conor's silky voice
that he deserves a rest — and so am I.
He makes me feel maybe I've finally earned
everything denied me for so long.

Conor: Hunger

We were grinning like loons after the beach. We hardly spoke on the way back through the sandhills. It's as if we were feeling each other's thoughts. We just let the horses take the reins and amble home.

I'd already made up salad sandwiches – since she's part rabbit. I was dying to touch her, but nothing was going to happen until we'd eaten, so I wolfed down my food. All of a sudden she began to talk like I've never heard, as if the sun and the beach and the gallop had set her loose. She had a few bites, but then filled her mouth with words. About her gran's place and her friend Clara, about the horses, the drought. Finally, she began to talk about her brother. She seems to love him, yet she's twisted about it.

I didn't want to rush her, but I had a place I'd been saving to show her last. I looked at the clock, shuffled my plate.

'I'm finished,' she said taking the hint.

'You've hardly eaten,' I said. 'You'll be hungry by the time we drive back to town.'

'Too excited, I guess. Maybe we can stop for something on the way?'

I didn't argue. I piled the plates in the sink and took her hand. 'Time for another tractor ride.'

'I thought you'd already shown me everything.'

'Ah now, it's always nice to end a good day with a surprise to top it off, my mother used to say.'

'Your mother was full of good ideas,' Diana said, looking almost as pleased as she had after the gallop. But then she added, 'Unlike mine.'

I slung a rucksack over my shoulder and we chugged off to my favourite place at the back of the property. You wouldn't know it was there until you were right in among the trees, a hideout screened by flowering acacias and coastal gums. A place that made me feel like a lad again, off on my own in the forest. It was private enough, too, for what we hungered for now.

Under My Skin

The tractor shakes me up.
Sun stares down in charge of every shadow
out in the open paddocks
where nothing can be hidden.
Dust swirls around with my anxiety.

I give myself the third degree.
Where will this lead?
What do I want to happen?

But suddenly we're cool among the trees,
dizzy with joyous birds,
blessed by shade,
a salt breeze from the shore.
What's been prepared for me?

Conor's shirt is open at the throat.
Red hairs like silky roots
make me want to feel how far they go.

I watch him toss a blanket in the air
as if he could conduct the choir above.
He smooths it down,
produces sweet temptations:
my body needs them all.

I rearrange myself to gain control,
my hands safe in my lap.
But it's too late by now. They're dry and split.

Already his earth's deep beneath my skin.

Conor: You First

Galahs clowned from branch to branch in the gums above. Sun stippled the ground through their canopies, making it look like my Gran's Oriental rug. I threw a blanket over some leaves and patted the spot beside me. Diana's knee touched mine.

'Dessert,' I said, taking out a box of gold-wrapped chocolates. 'And port to wash it down, a perfect dram for late afternoon.'

Diana laughed. 'We just had lunch.'

'A bite and a sip, that's all.' I felt nervous and hot as I twisted the bottle open and offered it.

'You first,' she said.

I took a long drink, feeling its sticky fire slide down my throat. I passed it to her and she took the bottle, sipped twice and smiled. 'Nice.'

I unwrapped a chocolate ball that began to melt in my palm almost at once. 'Here,' I held it out.

She looked into my eyes, as if deciding something. Her mouth touched my fingers as she leaned over to nibble. Then she began to lick chocolate off the tips.

That was it. I pulled her down and kissed her. Didn't stop. She tasted like chocolate and when she opened her mouth I felt her sweet breath inside me. The port had stirred my head and belly. When I put my hands beneath her shirt her breasts blazed. She arched herself against me. Then her hands found my groin. I couldn't take much of that. I rolled down, tugged at her jeans and buried my face in sweetness.

Rein Back

Galahs laugh overhead and call me back –
my pale, sad flesh exposed.
I gulp for air, drowning in the heat
and musky scents of someone. Is it me?

The day's too short,
already far too long for what I've done.
The wind swells as I rise, crisp from the south.
I zip myself back into my life.

Conor: Enough

Why did she push me off? I felt dazed as if I'd been ill with fever. I lay there blinking. 'What's wrong?'

'Nothing, it's not you.' She took a deep breath and tilted her neck. A ray of sun shot through the trees and lit up her face. She looked incredible. 'We don't have enough time.'

I checked my watch. 'We don't have to leave for at least an hour.'

'That's not enough time,' she said, 'at least not for me. I . . .' She turned away.

I bent over and took a few deep breaths. I could hardly move I wanted her so much. 'All right, we'll just have to find time. Soon.' I reached out for her hand, but she was already standing.

She wandered off while I tried to pull my heart up from a gallop. Finally I stood, brushed the rug down and packed the rucksack. When I glanced over she was leaning her head against a gum. Then I heard her whisper, 'There's never enough time.'

Desire

I hardly see the valleys and the hills
on our way back to town.
I'm in my mind, holding to the curves,
dodging images that bound across,
trying not to crash. And burn.

My muscles remember Misty's power,
the pure release of speed.
That part of me is calm,
the part that can't stop smiling
as if I'd swallowed sunlight.

My skin remembers, too,
a pulse that trembles from my toes
into the red centre.
Conor's hand lies on the seat.
I touch it and ignite.

I wonder, if we give ourselves,
do we 'die and rise the same',
as Donne says in his poem?
But after flaming how can we re-form
into what we were?

I long to be weightless ash.

I think I want to die,
but need to choose the place.
I've waited longer than most girls
for this sacrifice, to be laid out.
Time to prepare myself.

Since Conor tasted me,
I'm feverish and heavy in my bones.
Am I unfit for love?

Is that a way to race beyond myself?
My fingers itch to help relieve this ache.

Desire weighs me down.

Conor: Homeward Bound

The ute holds the curling road back to town. Diana's shoulder nudges me as we round a bend. We try not to smile. I'm driving one-handed and it's all I can do not to grab hers lying on the seat, doing nothing. I want it to be doing. The cab's still warm from the sun heating up the windscreen, although it's dusk. And then there's us, simmering next to each other.

We didn't have enough time, except to drive each other crazy. I haven't felt this grand since I moved to this upside-down country. And I thought she felt the same, but then she baulked. But what was that kiss about as we stood by the ute delaying the moment when she had to get in for the drive back? We both lost track of the hour, coming up for air as the sun thought about bedding down for the night. We panicked and drove flat chat as if we were late for the races.

We wind down onto the flat but she doesn't shift back to her side of the cab. The evening breeze stiffens and I close the windows. I want the day's heat to stay a little longer. Then I feel her palm cover my hand, holding firm.

At the Door

We're here. Now what?
It's eight o'clock. No verandah lights.
The darkness welcomes us,
the silence doesn't. What's behind the door?
I don't want him to know,
so don't invite him in.

Conor senses this, and checks his watch.
'Another one for the road?'
He tilts my face towards his.
'It's a cold drive home.'

I let him fold me back into his arms,
stroke my breasts, insinuate his fingers
where he wants. My skin rekindles,
who I thought I was implodes.

Hello darkness, my old friend,
My mother sang before she changed her tune.
My lover darkness, something sings inside.
I'm ready here at last,
knocking on your door.
Open. Take me in.

On the Other Side of the Door

The temperature drops.

I sniff the antiseptic air,
step into the Valley of Despair.
If Mum isn't cooking,
if no lights are on –
her car is in the drive –
everything is wrong.

Just my luck.
This family has a knack,
for timing and for blame.
How could I believe this day
would mean, would change . . .
dreams dissolve like pastilles on the tongue.

But their ghosts still hover
scented with leather, sand and leaves,
his sweat and mine.
His sweet taste's in my mouth.

The kitchen's dark. I flick the light
and read the signs:
an empty box of chocolates on the bench,
the table, bare.

I can't face upstairs yet.
I do what must be done.
I turn the hot tap on – full,
wash every trace of Conor off,
then let the cold tap run.

Lacey: Hello Darkness

'Go away,' I whisper.
My head knocks against the door.
It's bruised inside. I can't think.
But I'm still lying down.
The clock's green face gloats eight-fifteen.
I sit up. Then hear that tap again.

'Come in?'

'It's only me. I just got home.
What's wrong?'

'What's wrong?' My voice frightens even me,
a squeal like train brakes locking
too late to stop the crash.

Diana floats through gloom
and perches on the bed.
This wraith, my daughter,
hovers on the edges of our lives.
I can't face light.
My story needs this darkness.

'You left, that's what.
Philip felt abandoned,
relies on his routines.
I heard him in his room,
sorting things the way he does,
talking to his bear.

I thought, he's watching DVDs,
what he does when he sulks up there.
Later, I called him down to lunch – no answer.
When I checked, he'd vanished. Searched the house.
The front door was ajar.

No sign of him on this street or the next.

Of course I called your father. I was frantic.
He's somewhere in the hills,
troubleshooting on a job. The phone broke up.
He couldn't hear my message.
Sweet Jesus, do I need more trials?
Why do things always have to fail?'

Confession

Luckily she doesn't want an answer.
She wouldn't like to hear what I could say.
Isn't she exhausted playing martyr?
But I also know she was afraid.
I feel her guilt. It scents this cloistered air.
Does guilt always come with love?

Lacey: Lost and Found

'Don't you want to know what happened next?'
'Of course I do. But he must be all right,
or you'd have told me first.'
So logical, my daughter. So aloof.
So chilly in her love.
Everything is easy for the young.

'I called the cops,
who didn't seem to care.
They asked if he'd gone to visit mates.
"He's got no mates," I said.
They couldn't see,
he really could be lost.

There I was alone,
your father in the hills,
you down at the beach out on a joy ride –
your phone was off all day!
And Philip's walkabout. But then I thought –
He's at the park. That's what Diana promised.'

I feel her shifting on the bed.
Good.
She needs to understand the consequences.
My nerves are frayed.
I smell like burnt-out wire.
Why am I the one who always copes?

'I raced down to the oval,
and there he was watching boys play soccer,
yelling on the sidelines with the fathers.
I couldn't make him leave until the end.
Promised I would buy him a team jersey,
so he could look like them.'

'Is he upstairs?'
'Yes. Asleep.'
'At six o'clock?'
'Why do you sound surprised?
He was overtired, wouldn't settle.
I couldn't take much more. I had to rest.'

Her silence tells me she knows what that means.

Lacey: Message in a Bottle

I switch on the bed lamp. There she is,
face corpse-pale against the dark,
eyes like the bottom of the sea
where shipwrecks settle. Always judging me.
She notices the bottle on the table.
I know she knows what's in it.

'If he wakes by ten,
you can entertain him. I need sleep.'
I click the lamp and turn into myself.
The bed lightens as she floats away.
The door snaps shut.
For me the day is done.

No matter what she thinks, I've earned this rest.
Time to burrow down into my den.
She's on duty now.
I let that old sweet song wash though my head —
Hello darkness, my old friend.
I've come to talk with you again.

Robert: SOS Calls Only

Another false alarm.
Yet now that I'm home,
all Lacey does is complain.
Dazed with sleep she wobbles like a dog
that's run into a mirror.

'Who's to blame?
Blame your bloody God,' I finally say,
'whichever one you're worshipping this week.'
But that's always been her refrain
in every conversation.

'If I don't run the business, save enough,
what will happen if I die next month?
Try cooking gourmet, Lacey, on a pension.
It's not my fault the phone dropped out today.
SOS calls only in that valley.

This wasn't an emergency.
Tomorrow, though, it might be life or death
if I can't take time off.
Sunday's still a day of rest
in your church, I hope.'

Then the guilt douses my hot temper.
Philip's not as helpless as she thinks.
'He needs to learn,' I say, 'and take some risks.
He only wandered off
because he's caged here on his own.

Find a workshop of some kind —
for both of you —
or else you'll both go mad.'
That stops her in her tracks.
Her eyes glisten, catch the light.

I gave her paua earrings once
that made them shine like iridescent rainbows.
Diana has her eyes.
This can't go on.
All we do is fight.

I lean towards her, but she twists away,
and slams the bathroom door.
Good bloody night.

The Great Escape

At nine, Philip lumbers down the stairs,
like a bear who's been hibernating.
He yawns, his mouth an O
sucking in the overheated air.

But something's different.
He wants a special hug.
His face is calm, not dopey,
despite the Valium.

'So tell me about the Great Escape.
The Keeper with her whip and boots
tracked you through the bush
and drove you home?'

He laughs
because he gets the joke.
'So we live in a zoo. I love the zoo.
What animal are you?'

He looks at me with those liquid eyes –
my turn to laugh. 'A horse, I think.
But now it's story-time.
I haven't heard about your great adventure.'

He pulls me to the couch. 'I found the park.
I waited for the traffic lights to change.
I found the soccer boys.
I've never seen a game. A whole one.
It was so fun.'

'Mum went round the twist,' I shake my head.
'You can't just wander off.'

'I wasn't lost. I knew where I was.
And I was safe. I was in a crowd.
We were cheering for our side. We won.'

And then it hits me.
Philip's finally proud.

Going North

The long mid-year break begins in days.
Conor's going north. He has no choice,
he's got four weeks he can't afford to waste.
We're in the park eating a late lunch.
I pick at sour grapes,
grind the bitter seeds with Conor's news.

I've never been back down to ride.
When Conor asks I say I'm needed home.
Can my body learn to be alone?
Sometimes the nightgown sears my breasts,
the sheet floating down is hard to bear.
The weight's not Conor's.

If I give in he'll see my mirror self,
that slack sister who can put on weight.
It's my mum's fault. Her latest craze is cream.
Conor's voice intrudes,' If this is boring . . .'
'Sorry, no. I'm listening.'

'You'd better be,' he pokes me in the ribs.
'We're taking horses to some country tracks,
then we'll swing southeast down to Melbourne.
Depends on luck. If Quinn can win or place . . .'

'Can you just leave your property?'

'We've found a lad who's been with us a week
riding horses, mucking out the yards.
Maybe make a jockey Father hopes.
The neighbour's a good bloke,
he'll keep an eye on things while we're away.'
Conor taps my cheek. 'What will you do?'

A magpie lands nearby and eyes the grapes,
then stares at me as if to say, 'Well? Answer.'
I toss a grape and sigh. 'I've heaps of work.'
Conor draws me close but I resist.

'Meet us in Melbourne. I'll send you the fare.'
I hold my breath. This fantasy's too wild.
'My family's a mess,' I finally say.
Conor's patient tongue outlines my neck.
I let the heat between us melt my words.

Betrayal

We said goodbye for weeks.
Forever?
Conor's going, going, going.
Gone.

My first day of the break I'm sister helper.
Mother and son are 'doing health' in town:
three doctors in one afternoon,
two for Philip, one for her.

My reward? An hour in the mall
while specialists check Philip's heart.
He's big, it's weak and has a lot to bear.
And then my heart slips gears, hops, stalls.

Across the street stands Conor with a blond.
The building's glass reflects them and the crowd.
She's wearing boots and jeans,
but looks more Country Road than country girl.

Tall and thin, her mane of champagne hair
swings as he takes her shoulder
to steer her through the door.
What building is it? I can't think.

I change direction, hesitate to cross.
I'm melted to the spot.
Nudged and bumped, I stare,
even after they both disappear.

The light clicks. My brain refuses to,
then tells me what to do. Follow.
But something warns me not to –
the little red man flashes:

Stay in place.
Don't go.
You have no right. Give up.
Beware.

The Blob

When Philip finally goes to bed,
My mother watches movies in the lounge,
something horrible on demand –
rocket ships and blood –
anything that offers some escape.
It's been that kind of day,
scenarios of every kind:
The War of the Warrens,
The Boy who Ate Unley (with sauce),
Nightmare on Young Street 13.

I'm dazed, can't focus on my book,
can't lift a leg to exercise,
can't find her Valium.
Has she scoffed them all?
Tonight she's fed nervy Philip some.

The Blob is on, a 1950s film.
Teenagers save the world.
The hero's Steve McQueen;
My mother tells me that he's dead.
Cancer ate him up.
The movie's almost done.
The Blob's a greedy alien,
digesting whatever's in its path.
It fattens on assorted people,
pizza parlours, fancy cars and guns.

They – stupid *they* – don't respect its mission:
to absorb the world's impurities.
Finally, it's frozen in the Arctic.
My mother drowns the climax with her static,
unwrapping yet another golden chocolate.
She pops it whole into her mouth
and I can smell its sickly sweet.
I run upstairs to purge myself of her.

Midwinter

Midwinter now.
I rip the solstice off my calendar.
I don't need dates to tell me
how dark things are.

The parents hardly speak.
I'm here to guard the peace
in this coffin of a house.
I know I can't escape.

But today's a gift,
a stormy afternoon.
I cloak myself in rain gear,
a grim reaper stalking through the suburbs.

Thunder and lightning reign.
Dogs and cats scurry under cover.
But I'm a wild creature,
unafraid of drowning.

The world is glazed,
my skin is made of clouds,
outlined with blue-grey veins.
This is my skull I walk through.

Light is a candle glow
trembling in the rain
I know I can blow out
at any time.

Epilogue

Long ago I read these tales,
long ago in another life.

I shed that self
like a pair of jeans
gone at the seams,

dressed my soul in vogue,
the House of Diana's
all the rage for me.

Spring-cleaned my mind,
wiped each window carefully.
I see new text
shimmer between the lines —

that sliver of truth
in every myth,
a meaning small enough
to swallow whole.

It might be sharp,
but when it settles in my heart
I stay awake
to what the world is like

(sweet as sleep
and my mother's lies).
For I am pledged to truth.
Sisters, now I realise

your lesson is always the same:
the only safe place is the sky.

I Dream of Katoomba Falls

Another day, another crisis.
I send me to my room (without my dinner),
pop one of my mum's Valiums
and hope I'll have no dreams.
My pillow's rough as stone.
Blood swirls and pools,
and then there's egg-white foam
spilling on the rocks.

Suddenly I'm on that holiday
before we all gave up.
We reached a lookout near Katoomba Falls.
Dad blamed the mist for ruining the view.
Then as if to spite him,
the wind swept the mountains clear.
'Look. The horizon's smoky blue,
delicate as bird shells,' my mum said.

Against that sky the Three Sisters towered.
I'd read the legend about those girls,
frozen into rocks by their father
to save them from the Bunyip.
The father had to change shape too.
But at least a lyrebird can fly.
Then we're standing on wet stones
with scruffy orange skin. The Cascades.

Philip wants to touch the grinning cracks.
He splashes in, Mum screams and slips,
breaks her ankle. Then Dad swears.
I never reached the Falls,
but feel they're somewhere near.
Should I go over now,
finally fill my eyes and ears with foam,
think nothing but water?

Plateau

Dear Lord
I swear I have not sinned.
Nothing has passed my lips today
but lettuce leaves for lunch,
three green beans and a tofu square
for dinner, two glasses of water.

I nibbled from a tiny plate –
the portions look bigger – swept some in my lap.
In my pants are many pockets,
a sign of your bounty.
Zippers to seal the secret stains.

I have read the lives of saints
in the women's magazines.
They diet not to glorify your name,
only themselves. The perfection I seek
reveals your grand design – the essential female form.

I pray, melt flesh from my bones.
I cannot bear this hell
that has frozen over.
Can't you see my mouth
pressed against the ice?

Give us this day our daily loss.
Lead us not into temptation
but free us from frustration.

I accept this trial.
I am no lily of the field, mere decoration.
I suffer to create my form, my art.
I have fasted for forty days and nights
in my desert room.

Look, the moon approves.
She has slimmed to a crescent above the clouds.
Her halo beckons like a needle's eye.
I will make you a bargain, Lord.
I will grow so thin
I can pass through.

Then I'll deserve heaven.

Full Stop

I love this feeling of not being full.
I'm finally free and easy.
Is this a message from above, this pause?
Everything that happens has a meaning,
so my Mum sings. But this is all my fault
or else my victory.

She noticed that the pads were still unwrapped,
changed the subject, asking about Conor.
I told her we were finished. Over.
Period. She seemed relieved.

Was this a mother–daughter talk
without the detail?
But I can hear her think:
'A grandchild? That's the last thing I need,
with Philip still at home.'

Sorry, Mother Martyr,
I didn't do this for you.
There's more than one way to be born again,
and to be saved.

Sorry, Mother Moon,
first and purest model,
though I've danced to your rhythms,
I'm no longer your slave.

At last I realised what had to be.
I fasted as required,
I shut myself up tight.
I prayed, 'Obey me, body,'
and it did.

In Memoriam

After I'm dust, Mother,
after you scatter me from the beach
where Philip and I used to play
(write yourself a note, or you'll forget),
after my ash mingles with sun and spray,
indestructible now, eternally light –

drive home, tidy up,
throw an onion in the pot,
make believe you're cooking –
let domesticity flavour the air.

I imagine this scene:
Philip fumbles with Lego,
Big Forever Baby, the son and heir,
wondering where I am.
My one regret: deserting him.

I've left a letter, though,
for his sitter to read.
When she comes, let the two of them grieve.
Take a break. Have a Kit Kat or three.
Get your hair done.

At the beauty salon
flip through your favourite magazines
and presto: there I am.

'Exclusive Interview with Artemis'
(not her real name) –
'The Incredible Shrinking Girl,
a Model for her time.'
Read on and judge, then have your say
at www.beperfect.com.

At first you won't spot me, lured by juicier fare.
'Star Opens Up on Battle with Booze and Drugs',
or 'Shock Weight Gain for Oscar Hope',
or 'Fitness Guru Bashes Pregnant Diva
for Chocolate Spree'. But as you flip
past 'Vegetarian Starlet Anorexic'

something about my eyes will tempt you back –
their blue-green wash,
that sea over the rocks where I dissolved.
And you're sucked in:
your last chance to find out who I am.

Q: Tell us, Artemis, why did you leave school?

A: The usual fear and loathing in the halls:
cliques, bullies, haughty slimline girls,
sports-mad Aussie blokes strutting their stuff,
nerds and fatties cringing in the nooks
and crannies of the day, terrified.
The common herd hoping to slip by.

Q: What were your marks?

A: Biology and English were my strengths
so I combined the two in this project:
Experiment, Case Study, True Story.

Q: Your ultimate goal?

A: A body to match my soul.
To be the lightest being on earth
to still draw breath.

Q: What did your teachers say?

A: They didn't notice. Anyway,

counsellors tell us to aim for the stars,
so I have. After my death
I'll ascend above the rest,
become a heavenly body
like the classical moon. Glance up.
Even during the day we make an impression.
I am that pure Idea, a self-made Myth.

Mother, do you understand?
Look at me now with wonder.
How high and terrible
is your daughter!

Absolute Zero

'...the lowest temperature theoretically attainable, at which the particles constituting matter would be in the lowest energy states available.'

Naked on top of the sheets
I'm laid out in my final form.
Nothing moves but eyes beneath the lids,
a pulse at the wrist, slight swell of the breast.
Frozen in time, no more loss or gain –
this is what balance means.

A breeze flutters the curtains,
pure gauze fit to wrap me in.
Once I would have been chilled with so little flesh
but I've grown strong,
colder with my purpose.
My skin's a film of ice over my bones.

Look through and see the perfect frame,
every joint and ligament, arteries and veins.
I'm open for inspection,
a new museum feature,
a map of ideal woman,
eternal as water.

Vanishing Point

Rare as snow in the hills,
I drift past and you gaze
at my lightness and grace.
You glimpse the world through me.

Filter and sieve, I refine.
I am mercury, the first matter,
transmuting base flesh to gold,
the purest grams.

Rarefy is a word I found
that distils my heart.
I love what I am
now I am what I love –
nothing but the essential,
free of impurities.

Bones hold up a silken tent of skin
dusted with down.
My eyes are frosty skies.
That's all the description you need.

Nothing more to add to my story,
compressed to a point
with its own meaning,
a hole in the ice
into which I can vanish.

Safe on the shore in the cleansing wind,
admire me as the temperature drops.
Now do you see the perfection of zero?
Every time you shiver,
remember me.

Part Two: Plateau

Light

Slips between the blinds,
slithers to my bed and strikes.
I'm stung back to life.

Heart to Heart

Where am I?

Here.

Where's here?

See over there?

What? The chair?
My books, my mother's shawl.

Yes, you know.
You're in the hospital.
They brought you back.

From where?
Sleep?

The deepest kind,
the one you want – still.

Who are you to tell me
what I want?

You know, you do.

My head feels thick.

That's the wall
of blood and brick
you built to keep them out.

Who?

Them. All.

Does that include... ?

> *All. Remember.*
> *There's no pain in peace,*
> *no want or need.*

You won't let me forget?

> *I'm always here,*
> *the sea in your ear's shell.*

Help me not to need.

> *It's you who need*
> *some meaning.*
> *You chose what.*

Did I? What's my plan?

> *Keep your mouth shut.*
> *You can do it again.*

Can I be that strong?

> *Of course, it won't take long.*

Awakening

'You're up? Good. How about some breakfast?'
Nurse hauls the blinds. A winter sun glares in.
She's looks sexy in that uniform.
I can't turn much, hooked to Mother Drip.
Some formula to help me grow up big –
and they'd say strong.

'No breakfast.' Whose voice is that?
I sound like a dog that's howled too much.

'You have to try to eat.'

'Why?' A simple question.

'Your doctors say you must.' A dumb answer.
She wheels a tray across the bed.
I look into a bowl with something grey –
some former patient's brains?

'Your Mum's still here.
She spent the night sleeping in a chair.'

Where's Dad and Philip? Home alone together?
Has the earth shifted on its axis?

Nurse pats my hand. I hate fake sympathy.
I pull mine back as if she were infected.
But she won't be denied. 'Your Mum's upset.'

That sounds like her.

'Come on now, eat. At least a taste.
Your Mum is in the cafeteria.
She'll be up soon. Try for her.'

I almost laugh. Eat for her? My mother?

Nurse unwraps a spoon, her choice of weapons.
but I know how to wield them too.
I take it, dip, then stop, gaze in her eyes.
'Can I have toast instead? I like that more.'

She chirps, 'Of course,' and bustles out the door.
Now that was easy.
I scoop cereal into a napkin,
lean out of bed and toss it in the bin.

No Brakes

I feel drugged by sleep,
swim back to that day
across a gentle ocean, turquoise blue,
no ripples. Conor's beach.

What's that on the chair?
Plastic cows and horses,
corralled to keep them safe.
Philip. He's been here.

And I didn't wake?
He was that quiet?
This must be another drama.
Will my body know the part?

I close my eyes again and drift.
Feel the wind's breath, hear leather creak,
smell sweet rot, seaweed.
Someone speaks. The waves shush.

He wipes sweat from his face. And mine.
The sun rocks on past noon.
We're hot and wet, hungry.
Is it too late?

My heart quickens, takes three steps,
four, six, eight,
then bolts. I can't pull up.
No brakes.

They Say

It's after ten. Another nurse appears.
This one's done in grey –
coordinated eyes, teeth, hair.
Her sharp face is unlined, the hair pulled back.
Is that her way to save on facelifts?
A bun clings to her nape like a tumour.

This light reveals too much. Her faint beard glints.
I can't help being honest and too clever.
They always said I was. *They* –
Parents, teachers, kids – Elisavetta,
my last best friend at school. We were fourteen
and knew we were soul sisters from the first.

We shared our dreams, watched the Alpha girls
crack the whip of fashion. Still we were the chosen,
marked out for greater things.
I would be a teacher, she a dancer,
although she couldn't tell her family.
They were strict and didn't know much English.

We lived our lives together on the sly,
me studying, she practising at school,
until glandular fever hit her hard.
Three months she stayed at home.
Set adrift, I had to find a lifeline –
the lightest bodies are the ones they save.
They are those girls who love to make the rules
about who floats or sinks.

Good with words, and just slim enough,
I was welcomed in as unpaid tutor.
But they wanted more. They wanted secrets.
I traded off Elisavetta's life.
When she returned I hardly recognised her,

a peasant girl, puffing up the stairs,
who'd soon look like her mother —
that had to be a fate worse than death.
She'd have to know I couldn't really know her.
Which was worse? Betrayal or indulgence?

Greybeard cranks the bed and then she says,
'Your family's here. You were asleep before.
Can they come in?'
This time, I'm lost for words.

Brother

I see Philip first.
He's closest, leaning over
to see if I'm alive.

His eyes seem darker –
no longer sweet and liquid –
cloudy with fear.

A strand of rusty hair's stuck to his lip.
He wears his favourite tee – the Hulk.
His shiny skin smells of jasmine soap.

His mouth opens.
I can't bear to hear,
put a finger to my lips.

He hesitates,
but then swoops down
and hugs me hard.

Mother

She's quiet, but
she's never quiet.
Philip talks and she watches,
never takes her eyes off me.

Her eyes are blue and green like mine.
Mine are hers.
Grey's sifting through her hair.
When did that happen?

Once it looked like sandalwood
with sunrays streaking through,
and smelled of roses.
She's crumpled up now, shrunken.

She's in a faded skirt,
the black wool she only wears at home.
Why didn't she change?
She looks as if she's living on the streets.

The shawl on the armchair
I gave her for a gift –
blood-red cotton sewn with mirrors.
Most have fallen off.

She knows I'm watching, too.
When Philip pauses,
she finally rises, comes over,
speaks.

Father

He's lost. We're all here
and he doesn't know where
to put himself.

When he came in he hugged me after Philip.
Close up, I see now how alike they are,
the same soft needy eyes.

But first he patted Philip on the back
to ask for room.
He called him 'son'.

He's standing near the window now,
keeping light from shining in my face.
I can't see his,
only shadows.

He slips his hands into his pockets,
pulls them out,
puts them back,
checks his keys.

He's taking stock of solid things,
my father,
what he can touch and see.

What does he make of me?

Lacey and Robert: It Takes Two

There's our darling daughter,
our darling, dying daughter,
our pale experiment in parenting.

The blanket's almost flat.
It's hard to trace a body underneath,
one made of flesh and bone.

When she collapsed at home,
we called the ambulance.
The paramedics saved her.

They tell us she'll recover.
From what exactly?
Of course she's sick.

We all belong in hospital.
Our household throbs at night
like a racing heart.

Philip, for all his fits,
is blessedly the same.
She lets him hug her.

Will the doctor know a cure?
She wants to see us both
to settle the score.

Do we care who's to blame?
Diana's here,
our second-born, our first hope.

Our princess with the sea-green eyes.

Boredom

'You're white as flour,' doctor says.
He writes a recipe so I'll improve.
'Stir up feelings, add some sugar,
yeasty anger, let her rise, then bake.'
It's hot in this oven of a place.
Can you burn with ennui?
Freed at last from my umbilical,
I prowl this wing, snoop in other rooms.

A withered man's the centre of attention,
growling orders at his lumpy wife
who arranges flowers, bumps the vase,
spills water on the sheet.
Nothing's under her control
except her hair, permed in silver coils.
The daughter's bored, immersed in magazines.
Two grandchildren spread Lego on the floor.

Next a teenage girl in slinky shift
touches up her makeup as a man —
her uncle or her lover? — saunters in.
He's wearing a dark suit —
for work or for a morning funeral?
She pats the bed beside her,
sees me staring, glares with black-rimmed eyes,
and pulls the curtain round.

My mother's not arriving until four.
I've finished all my books.
I have no one to call.
I can't endure daytime TV.
I'm out of tricks to make poor time race past.
If I die will I be forced to haunt
these lemon-scented halls as punishment?
Now that's food for thought.

La Belle Dame – Mariska

'Come in.' I see a woman's silhouette
against a wall before I see her figure.
Her bed lamp casts the shadow.
She's caught me spying, so I hesitate.

'When I arrived I looked lost just like you.
This isn't quite the Hilton. Come in,' she says,
'and we'll amuse each other.'
She's tall with the profile of a taper,
dressed in mauve silk – expensive lingerie.
She's wound a matching scarf around her head.
Some silver strands escape.
So elegant, I feel a surge of envy,
although her face has an uncanny sheen.
One of my fellow spirits?
A *Belle Dame Sans Merci?*
But she is ill, not her wasting lover.

'You're very pale,' she says, 'but it suits.
Here, come sit by me.' She pats a chair,
then perches on the bed, a butterfly.
'You're also pretty even without makeup.
Lucky for you. Such eyes . . .'
She sighs at a mirror on her tray.
'My husband always said that I was lucky
I never turned into my Gran.
At sixty-five, skin like a labourer.
How old do you think I am?'

I shrug. 'It's not polite to guess.'

'Seventy.'

I raise my brows. She expects surprise,
but she is lovely.

'Tiny as when I first met my Luke
at twenty-one, always his slip of a girl.
He loved me to the end.'

'Is your husband dead?' Should I have asked?

'Yes, he's passed on. Too much stress.
He ran a business, raced his dogs.
Always gave me everything I wanted.'
She glances at her rings.
'Remember this as you get older.
A woman can never be too rich or thin.'

Mariska's Secret

I visit my new friend again,
who promises more secrets.
She rises, shuts the door,
returns and puts her hand upon my shoulder.

'Smoking does the trick.
Cigarettes kill the appetite.
I'm dying for one now.
The nurse will bring it soon. I'm due.

I walk around the little park below.
Stroll with me.'
I nod. Even if it's cold,
it's better than this hothouse.

'There's a quaint fountain,
some shrubs, a bench,
statues of playing children.
A peaceful place to take your mind off things . . .'

Her husky voice trails off, runs down, stops.
We sit as if enchanted.
The shadows deepen.
Soon it will be dark.

Finally she lies prone,
begins to cough, feels for a box of tissues,
plucks one or two and spits.
This breaks the spell.

'Talk to me now,' she murmurs.
'Tell me something nice about yourself.'
What can I say?
I begin to spin a fairytale.

Diana in Wonderland

1 Down the Rabbit Hole

This will be my first test,
trial by inquisition
with a senior psychiatrist.
I forget her name. Is that strange?
But I already know the opposition.

My torturer will offer treats,
tempt me with sugary love.
Futile. Fatal.
What she doesn't know about my heart
would fill her next book.

And here we are,
a hall bright enough to be death row.
I refused their last meal.
The ivory walls glare.
Is it jealousy?

Nothing can outglow
this lustrous daughter-of-pearl.
I have nothing to prove.

The nurse knocks and smiles.
I open the doctor's door.
I won't have to say a word.

She will see.

2 I Invent Dr Head

'Hello, I'm Dr …'
I blot out the voice.
I'll give her a name.

I nod and sit before her desk
but she stands up and gestures to a couch.
I rise and follow. Sit again.

She smiles. Good girl.
I half expect a pat.
My mouth is dry from drugs
otherwise I'd pant.

'How did you feel when you woke up?'
  'Is that the theme for today?'
'Would you like there to be a theme?'
  'Well, isn't there always?'

'What do you think it is?'
  'Aren't you paid for answers?'
'Do you think I'm asking the wrong questions?'
  'Can't you say anything straight?'

'What would you like me to say?'
  'You're boring as batshit.'
I raise my voice,
lose control of my face.

Too soon she's won this round.
But now I have a name.
My Dr Head I'll call her.

She wants to pin me down.
Quick! Where's the phone booth
for a costume change?

Out comes Diana of the Sheets,
my latest character. Let the mouth relax,
a hint of drool's a nice touch.

Make myself tight as a hospital bed.
Ideas bounce off like coins.
How much can she spend on me?

Ensconced in her chair, this squat Queen Bee
wants to suck me dry.
I'll need to sharpen my sting,

sweeten my lies. I can hear her mind hum.
Beware, smug Dr Head.
This is only round one.

3 Game Time

Yet another session with the bitch.

Sometimes we sit in silence —
tick tock   tick tock.
Today when she begins,
I decide to bully her, hit back:
whack   thump
question   answer
without a net.

'I'm bored with talk,' I finally say.
'Where are those games they play in films?
What kind of shrink are you?'

'You want a movie star?'

'You want to know where the bodies are?'

She can't suppress a smile.

'Buried very deep.'
Advantage — me.

'How many are there?'

'How many do you think?'

She snorts at that,
a schoolgirl reflex.

'Well, I'd better find out —
to give the families closure.'

We both laugh. Together.

4 A Pack of Cards

'Who cares for you?' said Alice... 'You're nothing but a
pack of cards!'
At this the whole pack rose up into the air, and came
flying down upon her; she gave a little scream, half of
fright and half of anger, and tried to beat them off...

'I've got a fancy pack of cards.'

Dr Head sways across the room.
Today she's wearing plum –
a wool skirt, a ripe fruit,
she smells sweet and easy.
She is what she is.

I sniff myself and notice nothing much:
a vague scent of bleach, pine, shed skin –
dead skin already cleansed.

'Here we are,' she says
and pulls a packet from a box.
Hey presto – not a rabbit.

'You can play with these
and tell me what they seem.'

She lays the inkblots on a table,
facedown in a pile.
'They're Rorschach cards.
I don't use them now.'

'Why not?' I ask.

'Better ways to find out what I want to know.'
She holds my eyes as if she could stop clocks,
then sits without her notebook on her throne.

She'll let her subject play.

Somewhere behind, her other eye and ear
record my every move.

I turn card one and grin.
It's black and white,
a mask with spaces for the eyes,
a hungry wolf, shedding fur.
He eats us out of house and home.
House or home?

I take my time.

'My brother could draw better.'
I turn card two. And frown.
Keep silent.

'Nothing to say?' she finally asks
after five minutes, giving in. I win.

'She shows me a spider.
I sit down beside her
and say what she wants to hear.'
I cock my head and stare.
I can stop clocks, too.

'And what do I want to hear?'

'Let's see.' I flip another card.
'Now this one looks
like Philip inked his bum
and sat on our parents' sheets.'

'Ten points for novelty.'

I'm glad I entertain.

Should I invite her in
to that forbidden country
from which no traveller returns?
My frozen wastes, my sad geography.
Is that truly me?

My mind is jumbled up
with stolen lines from books and films,
graphics from the net.
I read and think too much.

My head is overripe,
splitting with words.

Tea for Two

'I don't eat, I dine.'

Mariska pecks at a slice of beef
that won't yield to the hospital's blunt knife.
Clumsy as a peasant,
I've finished shuffling mine around my plate.
I can't help but admire – even her dissection
of half-ripe tomatoes is genteel.

'What's the custard like?'

I press its jaundiced skin with a spoon,
raise my martyr's eyes.

'It's time then for our after-dinner stroll.
Nurse Spy is on the prowl,
so stay alert when you grab your coat.'

She rummages in a bedside drawer,
turns and holds up a cigarette.
'I'll bring my own dessert.'

An Evening Off

Thank God – whatever gods may be.
Mum called to say that Philip isn't well.
They're staying home
and no one needs feel guilty.

It's hard to act the part
of the repentant daughter.
Some days I wish for a restful coma,
free of the weight of 'must' –
in my mum's terms: 'thou shalt.'

Mariska's blessed tonight with morphine sleep.
She's like a famous Diva
who sings her aria of pain,
seducing all who hear.
The nurses always give her what she wants.

I'm left alone to think
or not. Not-think.
Now there's an excellent idea.

First Contact

It's night within this city
in name only — too much fluorescent glare.
Coloured signs flicker on and off
without a sense of timing.
A blur of red and blue
makes it impossible to see
what should be in the sky.
People are afraid to read the dark.

I switch off the lights, stretch out on my bed,
shut my eyes to study my dim lids.
This inside screen is full of phantom gleams
and pathways leading — where?
I miss Gran's winter sky.
Could I still map the heavens?
Her deep-space black was easy,
stars pinned on its backdrop.

No close neighbours, no polluting light.
Did we read the future
or only trace the outlines of the past?
I can't remember now.
My mobile rings. I find it, flip the lid.
His number. Did I file him under
Home? Work? Friend? Lover?
Should I answer?

No, I whisper, but my noisy heart
raps till it hurts, an insistent fist
making me let him in.

Tell Me Why

'Hello?'

I breathe. He breathes. We wait.

'Diana?'

Yes, that is still me.

'I'm so sorry.' That's all he says at first.

'For what?'

He laughs his nervous laugh,
reminding me of Quinn's easy puffs
warming my hand.

The phone gleams in the dark,
but there's no real illumination.
'I don't know what to say.
Can I see you?'

'Why?'

'Because I care.
And I don't know why . . .'

'You should.'

'I don't,' and then he opens up,
runs hard as if the words whipped him on.
I almost smell his sweat.

What doesn't he know?

Why I cut him off,

why I wouldn't call him back
when he was on the road with his horses.
He hoped I'd fly to Melbourne,
he had a win, money,
he would have sent my fare.

And then he didn't see me at the college.
'Suppose I gave up,' Conor finally says.
'I almost drove to your place,
but then decided, no.
Father tells me when it comes to women,
I'm not the sharpest tool in the box . . .'

That nervous laugh again.
He realises what those words could mean.
'At least about how to fix things up.
But you didn't want me at your house,
that much was clear, your family . . .
Please tell me what I've done.'

He stops. Breathes. Waits.
How long does each breath take?
In, out, in out.
Then there's the heart.
How's its timing? Wrong between the beats.

I feel my faulty heart jolt,
reminding me it's there —
squeeze, release,
squeeze, release —
a temporary rhythm that will do,
at least for now.

'Please tell me what I've done,'
he asks again.

I say, 'All right.' Begin.

Boy Friend

I clinically laid out events and waited.
At first he sounded puzzled and then pleased.
He'd finally figured out that I was jealous.
What was his explanation?

The blond, his neighbour's daughter,
home from Queensland Uni for a visit,
needed to renew her driver's licence.
He offered her a lift.

'I went to town to register our truck.
We had forgot.' And that was it.
Then why was his arm so familiar?
Was this standard Irish charm, just him?

I let him ramble so I couldn't ask.
He's no boy and do I want a friend?
I let his voice wash through the winter night
like the soothing rain that had begun.

Conor: Falling Back

She asked, 'Why do you want to know me?' And then she said, 'Sometimes I don't want to know me.' It's overrated, knowing. Better to be feeling, doing, moving. That's the way I try to live. Moving on.

After Mother died, Father drank so he wouldn't know, although now her picture is the last thing he sees at night, propped by his bedside in a silver frame. She's perched bareback on a Connemara mare. He'd smashed the glass in a temper when those lads got suspended sentences for killing her.

Even though Diana told me what was wrong, the last few months seem like a jigsaw puzzle with pieces missing. Still, she must care if she thought I was off behind her back with Tracey, who deserves a hurricane's name. One trip to town with her was enough. In a way Diana reminds me of Father, who always seemed to get lost in his own dark forest. Mother managed to lead him into pockets of sun. Coming here's been good for him, though. Now he's wrapped up in the horses and the land. I might be a fool thinking I'll make a difference to Diana, but her emptiness pulls me like a magnet.

I had this dream after we talked. I'm thirteen, back in Ireland on a holiday in the North – the Giant's Causeway in County Antrim. It's the pavement of basalt rocks that Finn MacCool was supposed to have made as stepping stones. He wanted the Giant Benandonner to cross the sea from Scotland so they could fight. The legend tells that when MacCool saw the other Giant's size he turned tail. After all his bluster, he was a coward whose wife had to hide him. Father and I argued, I can't remember about what. So I hiked off alone.

I'm standing on top of the Organ, towering basalt pipes that MacCool made for Ossian, his son. I lean over. Do I expect to hear music? Up here the hill has a spare hide like a horse with mange. I wonder what it would be like to sleep on the fur of the rocks below, but maybe it's the water that draws me. In the fading sun it turns violet blue, with darker bruises showing where there are wells in the ocean floor. I know how to dive, although the water is too far away to reach, even for a Giant. I'd hit the rocks if I launched myself. But something in me wants that freedom.

Gran: Dear Diana

How are you?

I was terribly upset when your Father called to tell me you were in hospital. He says you're getting better and that I shouldn't bother coming, though I still might. But you know how long and hard the trip is, especially in winter. I can't drive at night anymore. The headlamps of those bloody trucks could be flying saucers for all I know. I'm going blind as a bat, and my bad hearing doesn't help my navigation skills.

I spoke to your mother yesterday. She told me not to call yet, that you don't want to talk, but I'm going to anyway, as soon as I think you've received this.

Don't you want to talk a bit, at least to me? I thought we had a good chat when I stayed over. Maybe your mother's judging by how you two get along. She said that she was praying constantly for you. What could I say to that? 'We're all praying for her.' Okay, I had to bite both lips — and cross my fingers and toes — to keep from saying anything else.

No matter what's wrong, you're still my best girl and I love you, whatever trouble you're in. If you don't want to talk, we'll just breathe at each other over the phone. That'll be the most excitement I've had in years.

Love
Gran

Mariska Who?

She stands in the afternoon glare
staring into the dark.
After seventy years she still doesn't know
what I've been asking.
'Who am I?' she sighs.
Who am am am am I I

The why and how
hiccupping in her head.
How odd it would be
to finally grow up at seventy –
but she hasn't done it.
Mariska, a name like a peasant dance.

She's light on her feet. She's losing weight
but not by choice. So beautiful once,
but cancer's tipping the scales.
The surgeon chose the knife,
carving out this slice of life
in our dreary ward.

I'm in the scene, a bit part in her play,
the pretty young thing
old enough to be the child
she never had,
lean as the greyhounds her husband used to race.
No space for anyone else.

Now greedy cells crowd out regrets and yet –
'How did I get to be so old?'
the mirror asks. 'How did I wind up here
without a child like you to leave behind
as handsome as I was?'
Handsome is as handsome does.

She flaps her hand behind her back,
still facing the window.
I'm her only audience now.
'I think I finally know.'
Her breath fogs the pane
as she whispers to herself.
Past her wispy head,
sun glazes the ocean –
oil on water set alight,
burning down to dusk.

Fed Up

Fed up with questions and with Dr Head.
I'm bored with mealtimes and my Hanseling.
I drop some crumbs, which lead them where I want —
this wilderness where everyone's the same,
fat enough to be some witch's feast.

Philip's here with Mum. She pops downstairs —
for snacks of course. He rattles off his news.
Saturdays he still goes to the park.
Dad takes him to the soccer games,
he gets to wear his jersey. He seems happy,
except he wants me home.

He asks me now, 'When will you come home?'
I can't bear that refrain.
'Tell *me* a story now,' I say.
He laughs and yet his eyes are huge with want.
I could fall in. I lie back, choose my dark.

So many riddles down the hole to solve.
I have to run —no time, no time. Tick-tock.
What are the dangerous things to eat and drink?
Philip shoots up tall.
I sip a potion, shrink,
but everywhere temptations grin and wink.

And then I'm drowning in a pool of tears.
I can't speak when my tongue has swelled with salt.
But Philip finds a party. We sip tea,
and I curl up inside a pot of sleep.
Then someone's temper flares.
The Queen Bee summons me. I must explain.
I speak one word but then she says, *Enough.*
Guilty as charged. Agreed.

Wake up, wake up, the clock sighs.
Philip's tickling my cheek.
I'm tangled on a lump of sheets.
'Wake up, Mum has the snacks.'

Firewater

'See what you have done!' she screamed. 'In a minute I shall melt away.'
Wicked Witch of the West

Conor's coming today.
What will I say?
'Why are you here?'
Don't show your fear.
Don't look.
I love and hate my silhouette.
Don't touch.
I might bite off your hand.

Don't burns like a shot
of tequila in my gut.
No's in my mouth —
bitter lemon and salt.
I shiver,
hugging my bones.
Alone Alone
I chose what I've become.

The blind blinks in the wind.
I flip it up and bathe in fire.
Windows are the world's eyes,
looking out, looking in.
I'm Dorothy without a home
but warm, finally warm.
A stroke of luck,
this sun.

Somewhere below the ice
something begins to shift.
What presses on my heart?
Am I a witch in heat without the blood?
Can dreams alone raise the temperature?

Dr Head asked me about stress.
That's not what caused this fever
I never want to drop.

Voices down the hall!
When he walks in, my wizard,
his eyes undress my soul.
Is this magic real?
What's left? What's left
begins to simmer.
Bubbles rise to my mouth and pop –
Yes Yes Yes

Conor: Talk to Me

Was she always this small? She looks like a fairy child swaddled in white, a wraith that might vanish if a mortal comes too close. Her eyes fix me and I can't say anything at first. She's propped up in bed as if on display. If she were lying down, I'd say she'd been prepared for a last viewing before they nailed the coffin lid shut.

I pull over a chair, sit and take her hand. Her eyes are not a child's. They're the murky sea green of the ocean floor. Her fingers are freezing, so I cover them, try to stroke warmth back in. After a minute, she rubs my palm with the top of her hand, as my old tabby used to do with her head.

I lean over and kiss her on each cheek. Her pale skin has a hard sheen, like the icing on a sweet bun. Whatever I've done, I can't have done enough for this. After we talked the other night, and she explained – as much as she was willing – she said, 'It isn't really your fault. I just can't deal with it all. You made me think life could change. It can't. After the ride, after we said goodbye, I walked through my door back into my old life, and time hadn't moved on one second, like a terrible magic...' But she didn't say more.

I can't think what might happen when she's out of hospital. I don't think she wants to either. She has to sort things. I said the typical, 'What can I do?' She shook her head, as if the question had no meaning. Then finally, 'Be here sometimes.' Whatever might happen, I can do that.

'Talk to me,' she says. So I do, telling her about the trip. As usual I can't shut up, but the currents in her eyes shift as I tell about Quinn's maiden run, about my plans. She laughs. I lean over, kiss her mouth and when she puts her fingers through my hair, no matter how frightened I am of what she is, I know we've got unfinished business.

The Gospel According to Gran

The phone rings and it's Gran,
whose voice strains up to middle C. 'Diana?'
'Hi,' I say. 'It's me.'

'Hi yourself. Is it safe to talk?
Are parents still around?
Doctors? Nurses? Rottweilers?'

'All clear. It's only nine o'clock. I'm free.'

'Now that's a claim. Who's ever free?'

'I don't need topics to debate.'

'I thought I always kept you on your toes,'
she says in her mock-offended voice.

'I'd prefer to fail all on my own,'
but I can't keep from laughing.

'It's good to hear that sound again.
Should I tell some of my old jokes?'

'They make me groan. If the nurses hear,
they'll take away my phone.'

'No one seems to have a sense of humour.
And your family . . .'

'The shrink hears enough about my family.
We wouldn't make a sit-com.'

'Don't I know. Sometimes I just can't recognise
your father as the country lad I raised.
And the city wasn't bad for him.

But Philip came on top of work and worry.
It's been hard for you all.'

'Philip is as good as he can be.
To tell the truth, he's the only one,
aside from you, who knows
how he should love me.'

'Everyone who should loves you, sweet,
as best they can. But let's be honest,
Philip takes a lot of time.
There isn't much left over.'

'And if there was?'

'You're asking this old chook,
who's pecking out a living on a pension?'

'You seem to do all right.'

'I'm used to making do. But that's me.
What do you want to do?'

'No one's asked me lately
what I want to be when I grow up.'

'I'm not talking five-year plans,
though putting eating on the next agenda
wouldn't go amiss.'

'Gran, I get the point.'

'I hope so or I'll make you sit on it.'

'But what's the use of planning?
I can't abandon Philip in that place.'

'That place is home. His parents love him, too.
Don't be so blind. I'll keep on at your mum
to think about the future. Wake up, girl.
All that I'm hearing are excuses.'

'Don't try to be my shrink.'

Gran has to cackle. 'Hey, I'm just a witch
who meddles when she can. The chooks and dogs
don't listen. You're the one that I can preach to.'

'You'll have to promise not to sing the sermon.'

'Agreed. I won't scare the congregation.
So, here's the lesson for today:
get well, get that degree, and then get out.
Don't think so much. You'll constipate yourself.'

'Laxatives are banned, at least for me.'

'Don't try to be so clever. Take advice
from someone who knows things aren't perfect.
My car is ancient but it's on the road.
The trick is don't press hard; you'll flood the motor.
Give it time to warm and just take off.

Going Off

*'Off with her head! the Queen shouted at the top of her voice.
Nobody moved.'*
Alice in Wonderland

Today I'm confident,
could face a jury of my peers,
rehearse my evidence.
'Herr Dr Head, Madame Prosecutor,
my turn to set the test.
Fair's fair. I'll choose the game we'll play.'

She nods. 'Okay. Let's see.'

'I'm good with words. Let's bounce off them.
"All's fair in love and war."
Your turn.'

'I'm still in love and not at war,
but you should act in here alone –
do a one-woman play.'

'Then who'll direct?'

'This show is yours.
Don't keep me in suspense.'

'Off with her head!' I shout.

Her eyebrows can't resist a twitch.

I know I'm not the Queen,
but Alice with her nose above the waves
in a pool of tears. If I don't drown,
what happens on the shore?
I deserve some punishment.

Bed without any supper.

Cheat,
the Rabbit whispers in my ear.
His watch ticks
Despair Despair.

My head is throbbing with my dreams,
my bad and saintly selves.
I want to scream,
'Off with it! Off with her head!'

Sisters

A little nurse hops in.
I call her willy wagtail –
she swings her bum and twitters,
'Mariska – Mrs Dowling –
is checking out this morning.
She'd like you to pop in before she goes.'
She flutters off. 'Don't be too long.
We don't want to miss lunch.'

My mother saw me sitting with Mariska,
lounging in designer lingerie.
Deciding I looked shabby, feeling guilty,
she bought me a pale-blue cotton gown.
I'm always ready now to pay a visit
to the ward's Grande Dame.

Today Mariska wears a dove-grey suit
and matching cloche that hugs her shapely head.
She has no silver strands left to escape.
'Merino wool,' she says when I admire.
'Heaven-soft. Here, feel.'

'You never mentioned leaving,'
I say aggrieved. I don't mind that she knows.
In between the hours spent with doctors
we've learned how to kill time:
strolling in our park and drinking tea,
swapping books, fooling naïve nurses.
We're friends. Although we made a solemn pact
never to reveal our diagnoses.

'Well, I wasn't sure,' she explains,
'but then the doctors told me yesterday –
what they had to say.
I'm going home for now.'

'You're coming back?'
Somehow I feel abandoned.
Is this how Philip feels when I desert him
even though he's not really alone?

'I won't come here, my sweet.'
She adjusts her hat,
checks her blood-plum lips.
They highlight her tissue-paper skin.

And then she laughs,
full-bellied, frightening.
I can't believe it comes from her,
a scarecrow, or the pole that it's been raised on.
Suddenly I'm pincered in her arms –
such bony strength. What does she think she'll lose?

She sighs, backs off and turns. 'Here, for you.'
She plucks a plastic bag from the bed.
Inside, the mauve silk gown,
the one that I first saw her in.

I protest.

'Don't worry, it's been washed.'

'I don't mean,' I begin, 'I can't accept...'

'Why not?' She puts a finger to her mouth.
The lipstick doesn't stain.
'There's no time left to wear out all my gowns.
Besides, the colour suits.'

'But you're so much taller and so slender.'

Her pale grey eyes appraise.
'Taller, yes, but thinner?

The gown is extra small.'

She clasps my shoulders,
steers me to the mirror,
stands behind, hands around my waist.
I feel her hips through the fine wool skirt.

'Look at us, Diana.
We're like sisters.'

Something More

Everyone flies behind my back,
buzzing to the Queen Bee in her hive.
She knows about the hidden scraps, the purging.
Then there's the scales. My body has betrayed me.
Is it that I'm starving for the truth?

'I know Mariska's dying.'
I pace the office, can't look in her face.

'There's something more.'
She states the fact but waits for confirmation.

'Gran is dying too.'

'How do you know?'

'I overheard my father on the phone.
He wants her to see specialists in town.
Now my parents say they need a break.
When I'm released they'll take us to the outback.

Business, Philip, college didn't matter.
'"We'll sort it out some way," my father said.
"We need a rest, a family holiday."
But he's the one who suddenly seemed ill.'

'Do you want to go?'

'Of course,' I snap.

'You're angry. Fine.
What do you need to do
if you want to be released in time?'

She lets the question hang,
waiting for my answer
to blow it away.

Dream Bodies

'I had a dream,' I say.
'Philip's in the hall at home.
I know he sometimes peeks around my door.
He watches me as I exercise.
I sit-up, stretch and bend, wipe off sweat,
then stand before the mirror.

All at once I'm there in triplicate.
There's Philip's me,
who reads him bedtime stories,
who guarantees "Sweet Dreams."
That Diana is the one he counts on,
a body that he will always love.

And there's a girl reflected in the glass
I think is plump, but maybe not. She hunches
so I can't tell. The bossy one's the third,
a stylish dominatrix with a whip
who struts between the others, centre stage.
Then I snap back. Philip's in the hall.

And I'm the one still before the mirror
trying to focus on what's there.
I close my eyes but their voices murmur
that each one knows me best.
'The question is,' my Queen of Questions says,
'which one will you hear?'

Bare

'Have you tried talking to your body?'

Is she the one who's crazy?
'I'm not that lonely yet.
When I reach that stage, I'll buy a pet.'

'My clever one, let's call a moratorium
on jokes and puns.
Time's running out and you're the one with deadlines.'

I hate it when she's right.

'Since it – or they – demand a lot of you,
it's only fair to ask them to explain.'

I hate role play, and now I want to bolt,
but feel as if she's tied me to the chair.
My hands sit in my lap. They're bluish-white.
The veins poke out, indecently exposed.
What would I ask? Which one of you am I?
Philip's body's grown but in his head
I think he stays the same yet is that true?

'And you?' she asks.
What have I said out loud?
'You have a woman's body.
There's been a boy – a man?'
She corrects herself and wets her lips.

Conor's lanky frame slinks through my mind.
She's invited him into this session
without my permission.
Her head nods at my silence.
I hate that she might write, *Won't answer. Fidgets.*
Frustrated and blocked.

She's seen me naked
one way or the other.
I don't want her to know
that's what I fear — Conor and me —
finally in the dark
stripped bare.

The Subject for Today

'I brought a friend home once.
I made her swear an oath of secrecy.
Philip didn't look like *her* brother.

She told the class about him, one by one.
Never again, I vowed, until years later
I trusted someone else – Elisavetta.

'I told you once about her,
my last best friend at school.
So that makes me betrayer and betrayed.
The lesson that I learned
is be invisible or else be clever
and rise so high no one can ever touch.'

And then I say without quite knowing why,
'Have you ever had a ride in a balloon?
My father won two tickets in a raffle
so we drove to the Barossa for the day.
It was autumn. I was six or seven.
This was our hour alone above the world.
The wind blew cold and Dad hugged me tight.
Below doll houses stood in perfect rows
and doll-house people tended to their gardens.
We drifted over paddocks bald from sheep.
The dairy pasture still looked emerald green
and horses galloped as our shadow swooped.'

'It must have been so hard, coming down.'

'Everyone comes down. Our hour was up.'

'And so is ours,' she smiles, 'but we can sit.
I'm in no rush today. Would you like tea?'

'All right,' I say, and surprise myself.

Liberation

1

I heard the nurses gossip
outside my room. They thought I'd gone.
I'm checking out today,
discharged into the world to convalesce.
What did they say? Blind to my loveliness,
they only saw a horror.
I listen as I face the mirror.
Their drama casts me in a death camp story:
A holocaust survivor,
a skeleton. A walking cliché?

Before escape I go to see my doctor,
rehearse the nurses' words.
She asks, 'What do you think?'
We're in the Queen Bee's hive –
the last in-house visit.

'I don't know,' I say.
'I'm not sure what I see.'

'What are you looking with –
your eyes or mind?'

'Is this a trick?'

She cuts to the quick:
'Search the net when you're home.
Type in concentration camps.
Study the girls and then yourself.
Who do you want to be?'

No sweetness here. Navigate alone,
that's what she means. Fly solo.

2

I've seen enough.
My mind's become
a charnel house of images.

3

Are bones sexy? Upstairs I undress
and gaze at my naked body.
What would Conor see?
If I turn out the light,
let him know me only by feel,
like a blind man,
will he think he's stumbled
into a terminal ward, or a graveyard?

I'm terrified of his tender fingers.
'Pity me,' I'd whisper, 'I live by my ideals,
a martyr to the cause.'
'What cause?' he'd ask.
Camp images flood back to trip me up.
Teenage girls – pale cheeks, cold eyes;
no warming blood sticky with promise
staining their thighs.

(*No one gave us a choice*,
their grinning skulls mock my arrogance.)
Just bones, bones, bones of splintered lives.
Was innocence ever a defence?
Hope ground into powder, mixed with ash,
the grey truth of the past thrown in my eyes
to blind me to the present –
or wake me to it?

Images melt together in my brain:
the bed's heat, the oven's flash.
Consuming passions — hate and love —
Could I die from pain or pleasure?
Where's the choice if white's my only colour?

4

Back to reality.
Below, I hear her call.
Mother, will you wash my winding sheet?
Prepare a final supper?
How thin my soul has grown.
That was never meant to waste away
but fatten on its own.
If I'm starved for love, what use is being free?
I don't want my bed
to remind him of the grave.

But who will save me?

Part Three: Gaining It

Family Breakfast

On parole. First day on good behaviour.

7:30. Breakfast.
Eggs: Pass.
Toast: Pluck a slice — Pass
Butter: Spread a film — Pass.

I take a bite, chew to make it last.
Healthy wholegrains stick between my teeth.

'Bacon anyone?'
My father is afraid to look at me.

'No thanks,' I say,
studying my plate.
Then I glance up.
'But maybe half an apple?'

The giant red delicious in the bowl
gleam like the furniture.

'Snow White ate one that looked like that.'
Philip grabs the biggest, holds it out.

'Don't worry. It's not poisoned,'
our mother says to the tablecloth.

'Let's share,' Philip says,
reaching for a knife
and knocking our dad's coffee,
who inhales slowly — in and out —
as the stain inevitably spreads.

'You cut and I'll clean up,' I say,
mopping with my napkin.

'How about another coffee?'
Mum offers Dad.
'The pot's half full.'

He nods, holds out his cup.

Some one thing

8:15 My new routine, a daily walk.

And there's our door.
It opens on its hinges – in.
Its solid wood keeps the world out,
the street that looks the same.
No spell's been cast,
nothing's changed but time,
the month. It's August.
That's something. Some one thing.

It's colder than I thought in my thin coat.
These days I find it hard to gauge the weather.
But shivering or not, I won't retreat.
I face into the sun
that packs a punch even at this season.
I squint into the glare and there, up high,
a plane is scribbling on the sky's blue slate.
'Be first to' something. Then the words dissolve.

But there's one thing I know.
This day of hot and cold
is any day I can choose to be
one day at a time.

Conor: Spring Fever

The seasons roll around again and I feel like kicking up my heels like Quinn. He's gone mad, on a spring sugar high from the shoots that blanket our paddocks. We had to separate him and Misty, he kept trying to mount her and she'd have none of it. She hasn't come into season yet and anyway I was told when I bought her that she was one of those bossy maidens who never let a stallion near.

It's only eight but near the beach the sun gets down to business early, urging me to shrug off my jacket as soon as I start hauling hay bales. I've lived here long enough to know what that warmth promises, even if the sun hasn't got the sting of a red-hot poker yet.

It's almost nine. Time to call. After Diana told me they were letting her out of hospital on good behaviour, she asked me to ring – in a week. She wanted to see how she settled at home. She said she felt as if she'd been gone a year. In Ireland we had a horse once, Mr McGinn, whom Father had sold to a trainer near Dublin. Six months later we bought him for next to nothing because the trainer needed cash. When we put McGinn back into his old paddock, he fell straight into his routines, including nipping his neighbours, so they knew that he was still boss. I guess those patterns made him feel at home again.

At least the weather's gentle now. Diana's got so little meat on her bones she must feel every chill. I hope the month warms fast so I can take her to the beach for a ride. 'If I'm strong enough,' she promised. 'I want to be.' When she wants her eyes catch light like the sea does at midday, as if a mirror had been smashed and strewn over the bay. But I can't count on the weather being on my side. I'll just have to try not to heat up myself until the right time.

Philip: Megaheart

*'I shall take the heart,' returned the Tin Woodman, 'for brains
do not make one happy, and happiness is the best thing in the
world.'*

*Dorothy did not say anything, for she was puzzled to know
which of her two friends was right...*

The Wizard of Oz

I watch it again and again, my movie, my favourite story. Diana read it to
me when she first learned to read – better than me. I sing along. I know
the words to keep us walking down the yellow brick road. There are no
songs in the book. But the story sings in my head.

Diana bought the DVD. Now I can watch whenever I want. I like
adventure and action heroes. The X-Men too. They aren't the same as
everyone else. They don't fit in. But they do what's right. My friends
from Oz don't fit. They're missing bits, but Dorothy loves them just the
same. And everyone finally does, too. They all find kingdoms they can
rule just by being themselves.

Di loves Dorothy most, a good girl who never gives up. I love the Lion
best because he's big and cuddly. Di says he's braver than he knows, he
only needs to believe. 'In what?' I asked. 'Himself.'

Last night she read, the first time in ages. She said we needed a trip
along the yellow brick road. We got to the part where the Tin Woodman
tells his tale.

'Who's right?' I asked. 'Which is better – brains or heart?'

Di dug me in the ribs. 'Clever boy. That would make a good essay
question.'

'I want brains *and* courage. I'm always afraid of those kids who live
near the shops.'

'Those kids have no brains,' Di said. And then she hugged me close.
Her hair smelled sweet like caramel.

'Time for bed,' she said.

But which is better? Tell. You're the one who's smart.'

She looked into my two eyes, kissed her finger, touched the tip of my
nose. 'Remember this, Megaboy. No one can live without heart.'

Lullaby

'Close your eyes.
Say goodbye to Oz.
Sweet dreams, sweet Megaheart.
Please, dear God,
give someone in this house, this home,
sweet dreams.'

Return to Oz

I tuck myself in

One am. Done with exercising.
Done with exorcising
those hungry demons.
Time to feed on sleep.

Road Show

Falling from the sky
I hover, searching for the road
I travelled as a child,
believing that somewhere magic lived.

The story knows there's no place like home.
I know that, too,
and dream of a balloon
to float me back to Oz,
to Dorothy and Co —
her ragged troupe of misfits
off to meet the wizard
in the great City of Wishes.

And there it is, my lifeline,
yolk-yellow brick dribbling through the outback
of fantasy. I land and join the group.
They smile and sing. I add my harmonies.
This journey's what I want,
this family of hopeful penitents
who welcome in a fifth disabled soul
missing bits herself.

Too soon we glimpse the city,
our green Holy Grail,
a glowing undersea Atlantis

barnacled with emeralds.
The sun ignites towers, walls and gate.
We're happy to be blinded,
put on the spectacles,
enter the Humbug's dream.

My friends stay drunk on promises,
obey the Wizard, melt the Wicked Witch,
wait like patient children for rewards.
But even when the curtain falls
on Oz the Terrible — no fiery Ball,
no Beast or Lady, no all-knowing Head;
even when they see the little man,
his egg-round skull stuffed with lies,

they willingly accept the brains and heart.
And courage? That he divvies up
so they can play the game until the end.
Dorothy clicks her heels.
How crazy to believe that silver shoes
can take you home except along a road
that maps back to your past.
And me? I'm on the sidelines once again.

No land to rule, no belief to rule me.
Stranded now between two worlds,
wizardless yet wanting —
little brains, no courage, too much heart.
The Monkeys' wings disturb the air,
silver sparks dissolve into the dawn.
A ruby glow spreads across my sheets.
Does this mean I'm reborn?

Wired

The doorbell rings.
My hand shakes my cup,
tea sloshes over.

I refuse to rush —
wipe up the spill,
take deep breaths.

Patience is a virtue.
These days I'm virtuous,
a Saint Diana,

not self-sacrificing,
but blessed among the living.
That's enough.

Three weeks since I've been free.
Conor's finally here. We've only talked,
the phone my fragile wavelength to his world.

Will he detect a change,
notice I've gained weight,
trimmed my hair, blushed my cheeks?

Do I look less like a statue now
and more a mythic marble come to life,
allowed her imperfections?

Open. Chimes tremble through my nerves.
Open. Don't even try to lie
when the bell is wired to your heart.

Paradox

Don't think. Just feel.
His arms. Yours.
Don't think. Inhale
his skin. Yours.

Don't check your heart.
Feel his bolt.
You're neck and neck.
Don't pull up.

A paradox,
frozen here
with so much heat.
Our eyes burn.

Nothing matters
now but want.
We sway and spin,
falling free.

Where will we crash?
Does he care?
His mouth on mine —
the answer.

Conor: In Time

I tried not to hope. We stand and hold each other, say nothing. Just breathe and rock. My face is buried in her hair. I smell something fresh – spring grass. I stroke her arms, smooth as a foal's coat. We press closer as if we could claim the same space. Her chest swells with air, her heart tapping out she's still alive. And staying. All of a sudden I'm not worried. We gentle each other down. I'm learning through my skin this other kind of harmony. We want to move in time.

At the Door Again

Voices startle us.
We spook and disunite.
Take calming breaths. Look round.
The same house. The same door
as last time – centuries ago.
I hear her voice again – Mother calling.
I – it is still I – smile and say,
'You might as well come in.'

Conor: One Step

I tell her she'll make a good track rider. She's got nerve and touch. Sensitive hands. A lot of lads don't, think it's all muscle and bluster. Some thoroughbreds need to be coddled. If you strongarm them, they set against you, lather up every time they prance out the gate, find reasons to shy.

I suggest she come to the races one day, just for a look. And she'll be a help. When I'm off instructing the jockey, Quinn frets by himself. He needs Diana to settle him down with her voice. Face it, lad. You're hoping the racing bug'll bite her too, she'll love the excitement.

'If you feel strong enough,' I say, 'you can exercise one of the geldings next time you come. We'll gallop together to begin.' And she agrees, yes, she'll give it a go.

Her mother – she insists I call her Lacey – says Diana should build herself up first. We set a date a few weeks off when she'll come. 'At least for the day. This time.' As Lacey bends over the stove, sliding out fresh-baked scones, we smile at *this time*.

Next month we turn the clocks ahead. Already the sun hangs around at dusk, butters the water before melting into the sea. The year's slipping past. Diana has heaps of work to make up if she wants to graduate with me in December. But she'll need a break, everyone agrees. Since Philip's father takes him out now Saturdays, Diana's free.

Lacey pops three scones on a plate. I grab two, Diana one. She cuts hers carefully, dabs it with jam. Bites an edge. Crumbs stick to her lip. I want to lick them off, but only brush them away with a fingertip.

We settle on a plan: first the ride, then the races soon after. Saturday week I'll leave at six to be at her house by seven-thirty. 'That way we'll have hours. Hours to fit everything in.' I can't keep my eyes from hers. 'I promise I'll have you home by dark.' And she grins.

Groundwork

Conor gives me a leg up.
Hero sidesteps, pivots
as I'm tossed like a bag of feed.
I grab his mane with one hand,
right myself, find the stirrups,
sort the reins, shift my weight,
find our centre, balance, breathe.

'On a chilly morning, they're all keen.'
That's Conor's favourite word.
Quinn seems to understand and whirls
as Conor tries to mount.
They dance around in an awkward circle
till Conor barks out, 'Stand,' then softens
once Quinn recollects who rules this herd.

'Easy boy, now settle.'
Conor strokes Quinn's blaze,
rubs his palm across both eyes.
Quinn blows out tension, slowly drops his head.
Man and horse, now motionless,
a tableau in the mist of their own breath.
Finally Conor swings up on his back
fluid as an eagle taking off.

At last it's time to fly.

Streamlined

Fuelled with toast and tea,
my body idles in the bitter air
until Conor says, 'Let's go.'
We leave the undercover yard.
At once the sun sweetens up the hour.
We bob through pools of light
beneath the gums that line the track.
Hero's coat gleams like polished brass.

Conor says we'll work them at the back.
We rein up by the gate
and the horses shoulder through,
anticipating what's about to happen.
My heart does too. I'm riding a Ferrari,
built for speed, without a bloody licence.
'Don't worry,' Conor smiles,
'there's nowhere to bolt except in circles.'

The horses swish through long dewy grass
until we hit the well-used path.
'They've loosened some. Let's ease into a canter.'
And so begins this test for my new self.
I'm calling her Diana of the Dunes,
a streamlined myth trying to take shape.
I have to stop this dreaming. Conor's off
and glances back just once to check I'm right.

Hero leaps and snorts, unseating me.
I wind a hank of mane between my fingers
until he changes gears, I catch his stride,
feel that lovely moment of suspension
in galloping that makes a rider bend
into a shape that doesn't fight the air.
Anyway I'm finished now with fighting.
This morning I don't care there is no race.

Jockey

A bloke is mixing feeds back at the yard.
His trim hips say that he's a boy
but his broader shoulders say a man.
Conor swings off Quinn before he calls,
'Di, meet Eric.' Then he grins.
'Eric knows already who you are.'

Eric only turns his face –
the weathered skin's sandpaper coarse.
He has a cat's impassive hazel eyes
that judge me at a glance.

'Yeah, I had no choice,' he answers.
'This one can't stop rattling on.'
He stands and lifts each feed.
'It's made me think of quitting more than once.'

'Did you now?' Conor laughs. 'What then?
 You haven't had it sweet like this in years.'

'Not be bored to death, that's for sure.'
His mouth quivers in a Cheshire smile
as he calls, 'Catch ya' later.'
The yarded horses nicker as he nears.

'Don't mind him. Though he's rough,
he's certainly a worker,' Conor says.
'And he has a jockey's quiet hands.'
'You're training him?' I ask as I wash Hero.

'He did a course some years ago,
then went off the rails with too much drink.
Dumb luck that he didn't go to jail.
Now he's met some woman up in town,
who's helping him to get his life on track.

Father thought that he's still worth a chance.'

Eric tips the feeds into the bins.
He stops to stroke each horse's face,
telling them that all's right in their world.
For now, things seem to be all right in his.

Northward Ho

This is the season to be here,
travelling north back in time
before the heat gets serious.
The vertebrae of the rocky ridges
sharp against a sky so clear
my eyes ache. How could I forget
this avatar of every blue I've loved?

The country looks its age and doesn't care –
sixteen thousand million years at least –
artless in the drought.
Pockmarked gibber plains,
roo-grey humps of hill nudging north.

From our tiny car, the distant ranges
look like they've been skinned,
the scruffy hide spread out on the flat
near clumps of stones,
monuments to someone's dreams,
someone's self-betrayal.

Like Gran, this place won't lie.
What does it mean to teach?
What am I ready to learn?
The real art of survival.

Forward to the Past: Friday

Late afternoon.
We've been cramped for hours in the car,
but minor miracles have been performed.
Philip listens to his tapes,
sings hymns with Mum and even Dad joins in.
'At least it drowns out you lot,' he exclaims.
And me? I watch and wait.
This trip's a lesson in itself,
a family practicum.
Can I mimic them?

By five the light has lost its edge.
The sun mellows into the horizon.
As we near Gran's place, I hear the crows
keening like the spirits of the dead.
And there she is, pacing back and forth
the way I remember.
I jump out first, back to the past,
trot across the yard to claim my hug.

But this is not her body.
She's shrunk, too much like victims of the drought,
those bones and flaps of hide
littering the country,
for me to miss this lesson.
Her fragile cage might crumble if I squeeze.
She sees me looking serious and winks.
In the sky the crows wail out the truth.

After tea Philip throws the ball
for grandma's dog, collects warm speckled eggs,
does a great impression of a chicken,
makes us laugh until we cry.
It's hard to stop.
My mother's brought her own supplies for dinner.

To her we're way back of beyond.
She's cooking stir-fry pork and jasmine rice.

Gran lets her criticise her pots
and then we leave her to it, slip away.
'I never thought I'd live to see the day,
when you'd all come to stay.'
'Was cancer, then, part of your cunning plan?'
My words, my voice sound wrong.
I'm the one who's sick.
She's merciful and smiles.

'The prodigal's back home.
Anyway, it seems to be a fad,
a fancy cancer for my generation.
Why should I buck the trend?'

'You never followed fads,' I insist
and clutch her arm.
The muscle's gone beneath the flesh.
'So why start now?'

'Well look, it worked.
You're all together here.
That almost makes
this dying business worth it.'

I take her hand, a little girl again,
with a feverish heart,
afraid that saying something makes it happen.
Later, the night wind answers back.

It stirs to life the house's guardians,
a row of she-oaks. Underneath the moon,
they quiver like moth wings.
By midnight they complain like hungry ghosts.

Rain: Sunday

Finally the sky remembers how it's done.
At one am it shudders, groans and cracks
until the blessed rain escapes.
The iron roof quivers with the storm.
I turn, half waking, let the water falling
enter my dreams as if I were a girl
cocooned in grandma's bed.
The Centaurs are dodging distant fires,
the light spears in the hills,
stars sizzling down, molten in the heat
of some celestial battle.
I drop asleep and never learn who's won.

But overnight there's been some sort of truce.
In the dawn the earth's relaxed and moist.
Gran picks Philip broccoli – his little trees.
The sky's a flawless blue,
no birds of omen screech across our path –
all the signs auspicious for a journey.

Gran says, 'You might be lucky.
The native blooms only need some showers
to poke their heads up. Both sides of the highway,
Sturt's desert peas grow wild.
They're tough as my old hide, those tart-red flowers,
but beautiful enough to stop your heart.'

It's ten. We're softened now to say goodbye.
Hugging her everyone is careful,
as if she'd were a fragile plant
that's easily uprooted.
I wait to be the last to kiss her cheek,
rub my face against her neck,
smell sweet spice, sweat,
everything good that I can remember.

'Take care of this lot, Lacey,'
Gran says as we climb into the car.
The engine revs and finally we're off.
But Mum turns and flicks a switch,
ordering her window down.
'Don't worry, Helen,' she calls out, 'I'm trying.'

Perspective

She isn't pacing as we disappear,
just stands there shrinking in the brightening day.
She shouted something – 'Look out for those flowers' –
and maybe then she added, 'Look for me.'
I'd like to say she vanished in the dust
and saved me from that cramping in my chest
but I endure each second till the view
redraws itself as *landscape without her*.
The air's twice washed, there's little dust to blur
the country or the sky. Too much is clear.

Yet somehow I feel lighter
in this world of clean and honest lines –
the unremitting flatness of the plain,
the dun hills traced in finepoint,
a distant eagle an emphatic dot
until it dives, cutting through the blue.
Even random bones beside the road
can't help but tell the truth.

Can one storm change so much?
I know some seed will rot,
some will wither in the hardening ground,
but somewhere it will sprout and struggle on.
And dust will blow, the dust she wants to be,
the kind you never sweep out of the gaps.

Philip cries and points, 'See over there?
What's that? Let's look. They might be Gran's flowers.'
A grey-green mat spreading near the road
flecked with drops of blood.
We stop and my dad fiddles with the camera
while I take Philip's hand.

We walk and see that closer
the flowers stand straight up from their stalks.
Black-chinned desert creatures,
wearing pointed hats and beards
coloured in such insistent scarlet
you can't believe it's real.

Yet in the midst of faded browns
they grow where they belong.
Philip starts to bend and I say,
'Stop. Don't touch.
Just look and you'll remember.
Sometimes to remember is enough.'

Recount

I tell the details of our trip,
list departure and arrival times,
routes, distance, weather,
food gathered from the garden
and meals eaten.
Describe the prospect from Gran's back verandah,
the thumbprint of plum blue between two hills
deepening at twilight.
Conor listens to the facts,
laughs, clears his throat.

I try to conjure him
as he holds the phone to his ear,
the right one with a bent lobe
that wisps of hair never tuck behind,
then stare into his eyes inside my mind –
those eyes, their after-rain honest blue.

And suddenly I'm back inside the storm
that pounded us all night,
the chaos of releasing thunder,
lightning that split me at the seams.
For seconds, minutes,
all I think is water.

No one speaks. Who can?

'Come down,' he finally says. 'Soon. Tomorrow.
I'm fatherless this week,
he's chasing horses.'

I shake myself like a sorry dog
summoned from the wet
and say the only word I want to say,
'Yes.'

Outpatient

I've been out for weeks, but I come back.
At least three visits with Cool Dr Head,
that's the deal I made myself —
penance and parole rolled into one.
Tomorrow Conor's coming.
I'm terrified of leaving
every body that I was behind.
When I return I'll never be the same.

I can't wait. I can't. Wait.

But today I still can smell their sweat
and feel their bulk,
these misfit girls of uncertain size.
I drag their patchwork pasts around.
They drag their feet as I approach her door.
They'd moonwalk backwards if they could.

Someone shudders at these grey-faced walls,
the scent of fear coming from her pores.
Another hates the seductive doctor.
A third can't figure out which feeling's love.
So who is left to judge?
My hand thinks for me, finally turns the knob.

Rereading

'Who makes you judge yourself?'

It's comforting to know she hasn't changed.
I need my fix of questions, feel the rush —
defiance, anger, frustration and shame.
'Everything and everyone,' I say.

'What things and who is everyone?' she asks.

Ah, now we're on an old familiar track,
her tit for tat, my rapper rider rhythm.
'We've been through this before.
All the voices of the past and present.'

'So nothing's new?' She smooths her tailored skirt,
folds her well-groomed hands, sits back and waits.
And so do I. I want to search this room
to see if any time has really passed.

'Hello in there,' she calls.
She rises and I see her silhouette
is leaner in the confident spring sun.
She's lost weight. Why? Should I ask the reason?
'I'll make some tea, shall I? We still can talk.
Tell me what you're reading.'

I tell her I've discovered other versions
of myths I thought that I had understood.
I found the Ngarrindjeri Seven Sisters
who pass the tests they're set. And then she says,
'Rereading helps you discover treasures
you might have missed first time around.'

'I guess I'm reading back into my life
and out of it again — old texts and new.'

I take the cup she offers,
sip the rosehip tea and burn my tongue.
This is a good familiar kind of pain,
reminding me that some things still can heal.

Conditional

I try to sleep.
My bed is like a coffin I once thought,
but now, I think, maybe like a pod.
Philip and I snuggled like two peas,
when we were small, wrapped up in our quilt.
My pulse beats time – I want to stop the clock.

My doctor asked me who was in control.
Who drew those pictures in my mind
of hollow Princess Ice? Who made me weak?
More to the point, now who is it that speaks?
Almost midnight now and early spring.
Time to lose your selves.

The window's open. If you can, escape.
Less than human, more than animal,
my nostrils flare at what's in the air
and what's below the ground pushing up.
Colour soon will rule,
pulsing through the world's veins.

I know next month violent pinks and yellows
will stain our garden's shadows.
Now roots twitch underground.
Seeds dream of shaking off the dirt
and feeding on the sun.
Kittens twist in the womb.

I have to stir and stretch.
Pegasus arrives,
galloping across the Southern sky,
warm air beneath his hooves.
The wind chimes in the yard tick-tock:
soon, soon, soon.

Race Day

Race day,
first start for me,
my virgin trial.
Finally time to learn about this passion.

Last minute chaos.
Quinn's thrown a racing plate.
Conor taps another on,
greases every hoof.

Then tosses me a comb and brush.
'Make him look a winner.
I need to do the same —
a lost cause, eh?'

He disappears to change
into the part of trainer.
At home I'm grubby strapper,
the staff he can't afford.

Quinn's dusty from a lazy morning roll.
I unknot his tail, a russet waterfall,
tug out twigs, leaves, hay,
then spray olive oil to make it shine.

Conor reappears in stiff new jeans.
A deep blue jacket makes his eyes
surge like a troubled sea.
We load up Quinn, who prances in the float.

At last we're through the gate,
the car accelerates and soothes his nerves.
Swirls of cloud dissolve.
Sun's already panting at our heels.

Traffic, too much traffic.

Conor grips the wheel
as if he'd strangle it.
The dashboard clock ticks inside our skulls.
Quinn whinnies, shifts his weight.

He knows this trip.
Too long he kicks.
Out now he kicks again.
Now. Let me run.

Conor: Last Things

I hate being late. That blasted farrier's slack. Quinn shouldn't have lost a shoe. Thank God Diana was here to tidy him up. He looks a winner, his coat glowing like whisky.

Twelve-thirty and it's searing. The ute almost stalls when we stop at the last set of lights before the track. The trainers' park is full. I manage to slip in between two trucks, as always feel the wishes rise like bile in my throat – to have a setup like that, and the string of winners to pack inside. Look at that bloke in the silk suit with strappers of his own, and flashy thoroughbreds shuffled like cards sideways in the truck.

I back Quinn out of the float and warn Diana again that now we're inside the gates, she can't even pat him. I didn't have time to get her licensed. But she can carry the rugs and other gear to the stalls. I tie him crossways with ropes and look out for the strapper I've hired for the race. Fifty dollars she gets and earns it. I spot her and wave, babble instructions, then rush to find the jockey, drop him my colours, see what he thinks of the field, finish the paperwork.

Diana trots after, doesn't chatter, listens and watches. A quick learner, she asks the right questions. Wants to know. A race is on so I stop to size up the track. Last week it was good on the inside, but today?

'Does it make a difference to Quinn?'

'I'm not sure. He hasn't raced enough. Probably not. I hope.'

We pass the Winners' Room with its glass wall. 'That's the holy grail. That's where we all want to be.'

'It looks like they're having a party. Were you ever inside?'

'When we first arrived from Ireland, a new mate of Father's won, invited us in. You're king of the course, at least for half an hour. Free drinks – though someone like me couldn't risk a mouthful when I have to drive. They lay on platters of food – crackers, cheese, fruit, cold meats. But the best is the video loop, which replays the last leg of the race so you watch your horse win again and again.'

'I'll bet that never gets boring.'

'Just give me enough winners to find out,' I say, catching my reflection in the glass.

Diana taps my shoulder. 'Well, my Irish dreamer, don't miss this chance. It's nearly one forty-five.'

My calves cramp as we jog back. Diana can't believe how small the saddle is, black plastic with white stitching. 'Not big enough for a child's bum, more like a perch.'

'Exactly,' I agree as I check the girth. 'It holds the stirrups and helps the jockey balance. They're light. Staying slim is part of the job. But they burn the steaks and salad that they live on.'

'You can see their hip bones through the silks. I thought they must live on hope.' Diana doesn't notice she's touching her own where they push against her jeans.

I feel a tremor in my groin, shake my head, take a breath. 'They're paid no matter what. It's blokes like me who diet on hope.'

Quinn's ready just in time. The white-smocked strapper leads him off, escorted by a steward in a green hacking jacket. They do things right here. As they pass, the steward's grey flicks its tail, fine as fairy floss.

Right behind, a fiery chestnut crabs, pulling out the arm of its owner, whose skirt's already stained with foam.

'Quinn seems relaxed. You're lucky he doesn't suffer from performance anxiety.'

Lucky for him, I think. What about me?

Austral Young Guns — 1000 metres

Three-year-olds fired up.
Dead track. Suits a few.
The Mighty Quinn among the field.
Place a bet. Two each way.
Who looks likely? Number six.
Honest hope. Number four.
Drawn the inside. Watch him close.
Beaten last. Take on trust.
Bred for distance. Not his race.
Fitter. Needs to toughen up.
Worth a flutter. Not too much.
Forget the grey. He tapers off.

Pre-war summit. Huddle round.
Forget beginner's easy picks.
'How do you see it?' Jockey sense.
'Worries me, the one with weight.'
Trainer tactics. 'Settle fourth.
Relax a bit. Then make a move.'

Leg up. Keep cool, hold back, hang on.
Parade around. The favourite's wild,
begins to bolt, upsets the field.
Prance over to the barriers.

The crowd's on standby till they're off.
Loudspeaker squawking, 'Pearl jumps well.'
Then hear a babel of race names.
Quinn settles fifth and bides his time.

Who leads? Who's last?
Now watch the screen.
Conor's silks — his mother's pride:
green, white shamrock, quartered cap.

At the bend, Quinn works to stay,
turns on the turbo, shoots away.
The pack thins out and points to home.

Neck and neck, nose and nose,
hoofbeats, heartbeats set the pace –
a blur of colours races past.

Mighty Quinn scores second place.

Conor: Fig Jam

Our jockey hops down, slips off his saddle and goes to the scales. I tell Diana don't even touch a sleeve. Course rules until they weigh out. 'That's how officials make sure no one cheats.'

'Fig Jam.' The winning trainer's full of himself, puffed up like a cock, exploding with talk. 'Fig Jam,' he smacks the owner on the back of his slick grey suit, tugs at the crown of his cap. 'Fig Jam,' he coughs and spits, raising his arm in a victory salute to the crowd.

Diana asks what that means. I shrug my shoulders. Can't tell her now. I don't want her to think we're all foul-mouthed and vain. But I've heard it enough while saddling up, one of the trainers' jokes. If I have a win here with Quinn, maybe I'd be tempted to say it, too: 'Fuck I'm Good. Just Ask Me!'

Still, a second's good money in my pocket and the promise of more to come. I can see now that Quinn was a bit underdone. I thought, too much work during the week, he'd run his race before we got to the track. But at three now, his body can take more. And his heart's relentless.

Today, second's enough. It's fired Diana up. She stands with her face lifted to Quinn, as if she's warming herself with his fire. I notice her checks aren't pale anymore. Today, second's enough, if Quinn and I are first in her heart.

Someone shouts out, 'Correct weight,' and Diana begins to laugh, can't stop, buries her face in my chest. She feels like a purring kitten. I catch the vibrations, begin to laugh too, and don't give a damn. We stand there, trembling skin and bone.

This Is

His body slips down mine,
trembling skin and bone.
Sweat polishes his chest
and he sticks, for the moment,
to my back,
pressing out all my hesitations.

He nips my neck,
his tomcat tongue purrs inside my ear.
Now I want to listen.
I love that little *pock* our bodies make
when we separate,
he turns me over.

His fingers know good things,
tease and release.
And then the push and shove,
straining after months of preparation.
Win or lose,
we're finally in this race.

It's strange how passion soothes.
My mind flares up again and finally melts,
a burnt candle welcoming the dark,
this gentling blindness, freeing me from sight.
Last conscious thought —

This is what I am.

Conor: Being There

Time belongs to her. I feel her body beat like a watch, shiver out each second under me, seconds that repeat with every ripple.

Opposites attract, but she's the contradiction. Her skin, pearl-smooth but never cool, hot like the centre of the earth.

And she's no pearl, more my secret lodestone. Though light as clouds, when she's lightning-charged she has to draw me in.

And in is where we want, to help us both forget — inside and out, day and night, pain and pleasure. We help each other into being there.

After Glow

Night is kind.
I melted into its thoughtless dark
and woke with sun polishing the window.

I glow and so does everything around.
Conor's rusty halo makes him seem an angel,
the kind that should have been in Bethlehem.

His bare arm's draped across my chest.
I follow the ribbing of a scar
through the tawny hair.

As if it sensed the danger,
it stops before a vein's blue rise.
His skin smells salty sweet.

Something scurries on the bedroom wall –
a gecko's aiming for a crack.
For now, it knows where it is going.

Conor slides his head onto my pillow.
Outside I hear an impatient wind
flinging cockatoos into the morning.

For us, here, now, there is no hurry.
I stretch and let each muscle test its length,
relaxing into this day's new shape.

The Magnificent Three

'He'll do right by you, mate,'
Eric says as he nods at Quinn.
'He's got a fire inside.'

'You and him both,' Conor laughs
as he girths the saddle up.
'Maybe we should slip those chillies
you munch raw like lollies in his feed.'

We're grooming horses for our morning ride.
Eric helps me tack up nervy Hero,
who's had a few days off.
But he and Conor only talk of Quinn –
his next race, the proper preparation,
how to set him up for the big win.

'You eat chillies raw?' I ask
touching Eric's arm.

He doesn't look me in the eye –
never does – shrugs off my hand
as if it were a fly beneath his notice.
'Put's hair on me chest,
and where it really counts.'
I sense his grin although he's turned
to slip the bit into Hero's mouth.
'Got that?' he says as he walks away.
'Next time you won't need my help.'

Is he miffed that Conor slept in?
We heard him in the dawn
shifting horses, making up the feeds.
Maybe he thinks that I distract his boss.

His ride, a dappled two-year-old,
fidgets at the gate. 'We're training her
for a local syndicate — a double win,'
Conor says, 'Good money and good will.'

'Let's see what's she's got,
before you count your winnings.'
Eric barks out 'Stand!,'
unties her and then mounts.

Conor laughs, hops on Quinn.
Has he forgotten me? But then he adds,
'I've put a tree stump by the fence.
Eric's idea, in case you're on your own.'

Once at the stump Hero won't stand still.
It takes three goes before I'm up.
I know this is a test, but who designed it?
Conor watches, smiles and nods. 'Good job.'

Eric's jogged ahead towards the beach.
Conor and I trot in his dusty wake.
I feel a fire in my belly too
but the heat's from panic.

The sun has raised the stakes,
galloped away with the hour.
It's like I'm breathing steam
and the horses feel like they'll explode.

We crest a sandhill and as if on cue,
we all sigh and snort. The southern breeze
whacks us and the beach is racing flat.
We quiver, suspended in the cool.

Then without a word
Conor and Eric jockey for position,
the horses plunging forward down the track.
As soon as they hit hard sand, they'll be off.

Hero and I bring up the rear,
but both our hearts are revving up.
When the others jump from trot to gallop,
Hero takes charge, surges to the front,

matching them stride for stride.
Eric turns, yells 'Yeeha'
looking straight into my face
and Conor whoops at both of us to answer.

Together we burn up the endless shore,
the magnificent three,
huffing with our horses,
the music of our blood in our ears.

Conor: Gone Again

We had to be gone by dusk. That tug on her heart for home cooled off the day for both of us. I know she wants to stay but doesn't say a word, just keeps helping me bed down the stabled horses, whispers to Quinn every time she passes, even lends Eric a hand cleaning tack. If nothing else that'll win him over.

He's a moody lad, Eric. After all these months, I still don't know what makes him tick. Father says just leave him alone to do his work. If something's gone wrong in his life, it isn't our place to fix it. Maybe Father sees some of himself in Eric.

Of course Diana and I are back late, but no one mentions it. Diana's mother gives me a cup of tea and a caramel slice with a chocolate paver laid on top. Philip tells me how he made the cookie base. That brown sugary taste still coats my mouth as I drive home, but that's not what I was hungry for. I grip the steering wheel but my hands itch and only the balm of her skin can soothe them.

I come home to an empty house. Father's in Murray Bridge till tomorrow and Eric said he was off to town to see his woman. I've told him more than once that it was fine with us if he brought her here. Usually he just shrugs me off.

But yesterday as I was rushing with feeds at dawn so I could pick up Diana on time, he said, 'I can see she's got you organised already.'

'Maybe I want to be organised,' I laughed.

He closed his eyes for a minute then and shook his head. 'Maybe we all end up organised by a woman.'

'Worse things could happen to a bloke,' I told him as I grabbed the last two buckets.

He was putting down the phone when I came into the kitchen to grab the ute keys. 'Mimi's coming next weekend, if that's ok. She just got her roster and she's off.'

I nodded. That was the first time he'd ever mentioned her name.

'Makes sense to stay. She lives in Salisbury, the other end of the earth from here. That's where she works as a vet nurse.' So something's changed between them. He's lightened up.

After our gallop down the beach — and that grey mare is a goer, pushed Quinn into fifth gear — Eric babbled on like a kookaburra on speed. We talked the whole time we were sorting out the horses, making plans for Quinn and his new training partner. And when Diana was out of earshot, washing down Hero, he surprised me by nodding in her direction and saying, 'Let her keep on with him. They get along. It'll free me up some to work this little beauty. Won't it, Tequila?' The mare rubbed her nose against his shirt and he chuckled.

I told Diana on the way back that she can work Hero as much as she wants. It will steady him to have only one rider for a while.

'You think so? Really?' She looked disbelieving but couldn't help giving me that no-holds-barred smile that makes me feel as if I've been winded. I told her Eric agreed. Her smile flicked onto high beam and the air around her shimmered. I was gone again like this morning, when I opened my eyes and had trouble focusing on anything but her face.

So This Is Spring

So this is spring –
a season for ends and for beginnings.
The end of study, finally graduation.
My mother thanked the Lord, bought me a dress
for the occasion. Dad bought me a car,
which made this Independence Day for me.

But maybe Philip is the one who's grown.
Was it the camera that Dad bought for him
that woke him from a decade's hibernation?
He loved the word – photography –
the power to capture what he loved.
Now my horse-struck Philip wants to draw.

I had dared a road trip on our own
after late spring rain. We left at dawn
for Conor's property.
The wizard sun,
as we drove down the hill,
made his paddocks shimmer green like Oz.

On that first day my brother clicked so much
his index finger cramped.
Then he grew brave with Quinn.
He stroked his flanks, favourite-pillow smooth,
combed the nests out of his tail,
stood nose-to-nose exchanging breath.

Later Conor rode in the arena.
Fascinated, Philip crooned and swayed,
feeling every motion with his body.
Where did he learn that rhythm?
Like a saint rapt in contemplation
he became one with what he loved.

At home his pastel shapes jumped off the page.

Heating Up

Last night the phone glowed,
the handset hot and damp.

Conor – the drum in my ear beats.
Conor – the rhythm that rolls me in bed.
Conor – the name that whispers through my days.

Last week we lay in summer's golden bowl,
naked in the dunes.
Light seared through the glass –
his body's brand is on me now.

Tomorrow I drive down but not alone.
I promised Philip one more trip
before the New Year break.
Philip needs. I need, but I can't stay.

Can't – acidic word
that scars my heart.

Today begins to boil.
The car fumes in despair.
Air belches in the window.
My brother doesn't care.

He'll be with his new mates,
clutches his camera and his pad,
a box stocked with pastels, charcoal, pens,
the colours of his love.

We spiral down the valley;
the fresh sea winks between the hills,
but the weary gums droop overhead,
rattling in my ears.
I think of bones, of ash.

Suddenly, my nose begins to twitch.

Red Alert

We struggle up the last rise,
glide over, rollercoaster down
into an ocean of dense heat.
The town is swamped.

People stroke against the surging wind
to save themselves, clutch at doors,
gasping into bakeries and banks,
grocery stores – any cool salvation.

Past the last thread of houses
the car stumbles on the tar-blotched road –
bitumen melts beneath the wheels.
Already, I feel this trip is hopeless.

When we arrive Conor's nerves are tuned
as fine as fencing wire.
He gives us both brief hugs,
then starts to slam the news.

'The radio said thirty-five today.
They couldn't predict a day in hell.
Look at the gauge.
It says it's nearly forty!'

His voice rises. 'Father's up at Oakbank.
Eric went for tractor parts,
had a blowout, won't be back till ten.
No one's here. Now I need to leave.'

Then he explains about the horses
spelling in a paddock in the forest –
Hero and Tequila, that young mare.
'Too dangerous in this heat to keep them there.

I left her halter on. She's hard to catch.
Besides, she's had a week of forest grass.'
And then I know. He can't do this alone.
But Philip's wandered off to the stable.

I finally see him nose to nose with Quinn.
Around them, everything's in motion —
wisps of hay, buckets, whips of rope.
Together they ignore the vicious wind.

Another Great Adventure

There's nothing for it. Philip has to come.
Conor hitches up the float.
I organise bribes for the horses —
lucerne chaff and carrots.

But Philip doesn't want to leave.
He's busy with his sketches.
I tell him that we're on a rescue mission
to save two horses stranded in the forest.

We need his help on this great adventure.
He can spot for fires.
'Will there be danger?'
I nod and hope I'm wrong.

Pines

Impatient wind rocks the float,
pushing us to the forest gate
as if it wants to see if we survive.
The pines close over us and dim the sky.

The paddock isn't far,
but this track bumps with wizened cones
and needles crunching under wheels
like tiny bones.

The air tastes sour;
it smells like memories
that no one wants.
I try not to swallow down the truth.

We reach a second gate,
but even here the pines take body blows
as the wind rips through.
They wrestle and complain,

flinging birds from heaving branches.
Screeching flocks form and disappear
into a bank of sallow cloud.
And yet there's no real silence.

My ears are dumb.
I can't tell what I hear.
This noise is fat with promises.
Which of them today will be fulfilled?

Big Brother

'Stay by the float,' I say.
'Yell out if you see fire.
That will be a help.'

Philip shuffles from foot to foot
and grabs my arm.
He knows that something's wrong.

'Please. We need you here.
Someone has to guard the car.
Too many of us will spook the horses.'

I whine as if it were my turn
after all these years
to claim the centre of attention.

His flushed face stills and then he says
in his grown-up voice,
'I love the horses.'

I stroke his damp hand and lift it off.
'Come on, big brother. Please. We're losing time.'
And suddenly he smiles.

'We can't lose him again.
Don't worry Di. I'm bigger than you are.
I can take care.'

Rush

I reach the paddock gate.
Dense grass has jammed it shut.
I lift and shove,

then glance back to check.
Watchman Philip's leaning on the float,
one hand above his eyes.

I grab the halter Conor's left
and push into the whirl.
I know I must stay calm,

but somehow I'm too feverish,
too glad to be here now.
Every sparking nerve gives me a rush.

If I'm not careful, I might catch alight.

Prey

Whinnies carry on the wind —
the horses wheel and brake,
charge along the fence,
buck and fart but this is not a game.

The forest is in pain.
Gums shed brittle skin
that snaps beneath frantic horses' hooves.
Pine joints sound as if they needed oil.

Hero and the mare skid at the gate.
They hammer with their chests
but the metal doesn't give,
booms like a speedway crash.

They rear and drop.
Rear. Back up.
Oozing foam, they steam,
sides heaving like bellows.

Standing in the centre of the paddock,
Conor croons. Their ears curve to his voice.
He slowly lifts a hand,
begins to walk. One step. Then another.

They watch, shift against each other.
Far off something's gaining ground —
an army of dry leaves,
sweeping on beneath the jaundiced sky.

A branch spears into the brush nearby.
The horses bolt.
Like any prey
the first line of defence is always run.

Conor groans and drops.
Sweat cuts each cheek.
He sits and bows his head
as if he's stunned.

I drop as well. Feel useless.
The horses gallop in their witless circles.
Then suddenly the wind reins back.
A lull.

Truce

The day holds its breath.
Tormented pines flinch and still.
Gums whisper to themselves –
is it all over?

A breeze shifts,
stirs hair on my left cheek.
I can't tell which direction
might mean danger.

Heat drowns us once again.
It's hard to breathe.
I'm wet
as if I'd been hosed off.

For now, wind obeys the truce.
The horses stay alert,
lift their heads,
snort and shake.

I shiver too,
but at a wilful gust
that's like a ghost
panting on my grave.

Conor rises,
signs to me –
It's time to move.

No Lasting Peace

Hero takes three steps. Halts.
I hold a carrot out.
He leans and nips.
His eyes triple-check that it's me.

I sidle up, stroke his neck,
slip the rope beneath,
then slide the halter on.
Now I can breathe.

Conor and his bucket face the mare.
She tests him with her nose but hesitates
although she's jealous,
glaring at Hero as he eats.

Conor edges closer.
He offers, she considers,
dips her poll.
The lead clicks on the ring.

Her muzzle swishes in dry chaff.
She snorts and sprays.
Conor starts to sneeze.
We laugh together, glad we finally can.

'A few more mouthfuls,' Conor says,
'and then we're off. Let's not push our luck.'
He rubs the mare's eyes to keep her calm.
'And save one carrot for emergencies.'

'I thought this qualified,' I say.
'What else can happen?'
'The wind is blowing from the north again.
We're not home yet and there's a fire somewhere.'

The mare's skin twitches even though the flies
have vanished in the swelling breeze.
'And these two seem to know.' Conor frowns.
Hero whinnies, paws the ground and stamps.

Discovery

Once we leave the paddock
the horses crab and prance to the float.
Philip must be in the ute. Good, I think.
We need to load them without fuss.

Hero rushes in
to lucerne hay dangling in a net.
Tequila baulks,
but Conor has no time for gentleness.

I hold her head.
He stands beside her bum –
his palm strikes like a match.
One bound and she slots in.

We hoist the tailgate, latch it.
Conor smiles.
Even ripe with sweat my body yearns,
but he's already turned aside.

We both race to our doors.
The rising gale insists.
I look inside and my heart misfires.
Now Philip's run away.

Philip: Fox

The gums throw things at me. I toss them back. Now the wind tries to push me over. But I won't give in. I'm here to watch. Di and Conor can't catch the horses. They're running silly and won't listen. But I do. I can't see far. The sky keeps changing colour. Now it's like my fuzzy yellow blanket. No one needs a blanket when it's hot.

I don't see fire but there's something red. What's hiding in that bush? The branches move. It's not a kangaroo. They jump away. A little fox, with a soft long tail. Di says she's seen them in the sandhills, too. They shouldn't live there and they scare the horses.

Conor shoots them if he can. I don't know if he has his gun. I don't like things to die. I'll make it run. Otherwise they won't catch the horses.

Look at its staring eyes. My cat has golden eyes like swirly marbles, but not a bushy tail. It's brave just standing there. I'll shoo it off.

That's good. It's trotting now. But then it stops, not far enough away. It doesn't think I'll follow. 'Yarrr,' I growl and then it runs and I do too. I can't let it come back. The pines are thick and whack me in the mouth, but I'm a Hulk. I can push through.

'Yarrrr,' I growl again. The horses won't hear now. I'm far away.

Panic

I howl above the wind to make him leave.
'We can't search with horses in the float.
They're kicking now and what if…'
Words blister on my tongue.

Conor's shouting 'No' as I retreat.
'Unload them. Come straight back. Bring Eric too.
I've got my phone.' I'm pleading now.
'There's still a signal.

I'll use this as the centre, fan out wider.'
My words blow off in the gale's bad breath
that thumps the ute side on.
Both horses panic, trying to kick free.

They sock the tailgate, juddering the float.
'Go! You're wasting time.'
Conor wheels and runs,
starts the engine, revs and tears away.

The gunshots of their hooves
start to fade.
I turn and jog,
alone with my despair.

I want to scorch my throat with his name.
If I can't find Philip
I'll find fire.
I'm the one who deserves to burn.

Philip: Lost

I almost fall when kangaroos jump by. I've never seen them close. The fox scares them. They scare the fox. They've done my job for me.

It's noisier in the forest now. All the birds are screeching as they fly. I know their names – magpies, cockatoos. And tiny birds that swirl like specks of dust. The scabby gums and bushes crowd me in but I turn round and push. I have to find my way back to the float.

'Which way to push?'

My Nasty Self starts to shout at me. 'Which is the path? You should have dropped something when you ran. Like Hansel it would show you where to go.'

'I can be brave. I found my way to soccer once. Remember?'

'But you'd been there before. You're stupid, lost.'

When I look up I only see the treetops. The pines smell like the bathroom when it's cleaned. Smoke puffs to the left. There must be fire. I'll have to tell Di that I spotted one. I'll go the other way. That's safe.

'How long have you been hunting for the fox?'

'I can't remember.'

'Stupid. Try to think.'

'Don't call me that. Diana will come find me.'

I know this tree. Its trunk is bald just there. It looks like the top of my dad's head. This is where I'll wait. If Di comes looking, this is near my path.

'Yell, Stupid, yell. At least then she might hear.'

'Don't call me Stupid, Stupid!' I shout back. Now that makes me feel better.

Conor: Dumb Luck

The horses heave in the back like drunks. We almost flip over. When I turn I can hardly make out their heads, smudged through the glass. Forget them, lad, I tell myself. Watch the bloody road. It's spiked with rocks. A blowout now will finish us all.

My insides flare like hot spots as I think what might happen to Diana, to her brother. My fault. I shouldn't have let them come, bloody selfish dolt that I am, fixed on the horses.

I park in front of the house, fling down the float's tailgate, still each horse with a hand on their flanks, then unlatch the chains over their bums. They charge back, no time for manners, and I just manage to jump clear. The mare dashes off towards the raceway before I can catch her. Lucky the gate's closed. I let her canter along the fence line and deal with Hero first, who stands long enough for me to grab his lead. I chuck him into the nearest yard.

Now for Tequila. She's trotted over to the stable lean-to where we store feedbags. One ear's twisted back for danger, the other's forward as she sniffs. I grab a bucket and toss in some oats. Dumb luck is with me this time too and she waits for her reward. I pull her over to an empty stall.

Just as I start to unhook the float I hear Eric's Holden shudder down the drive. I empty my lungs as if I've been holding my breath underwater. Dumb or not, luck is with me again. We can search together.

Will I be three times lucky and find Diana and her brother? Why is luck dumb if it saves you? What doesn't it know?

Tracking

I lose myself in the nearest scrub,
the forest litter snapping at my heels.
I can barely breathe the acrid pine,
the crushing scent of loss.

As I expand my circle,
I scar the trunks with a pocketknife
to mark off what I've searched.
Then I realise how dumb that is.

A waste of time. I start to shout.
Twigs spit like heating oil
as I stumble forward.
Where would Philip go?

'Just look,' I say out loud.
'Don't think too much.'
I focus and among the trees
suddenly I can see a trail

hidden by the wild-haired brush.
I race and pant. All my senses flare.
Nose confirms there's smoke,
but not close — yet.

My ears go mad with noise
as flocks overhead almost collide.
The forest is shrieking for a way out.
I want to shriek myself

but I'm the only Search and Rescue here.
I have to keep control. Push on. And trip,
stagger up, push forward. There's a gap,
steaming in sunlight, up ahead.

Conor: Boiling Over

Eric's a country lad. He knows when the day boils over there can't be anything good on the news. He tuned the radio so he'd catch the emergency warnings while he was changing the tyre.

As soon as he climbed out of his Holden, he took one look at my face and scanned the yard. 'Where's your girl? Not coming?' Tequila nickered at him from her stall. 'You picked them up. Yourself? Then you're a bloody better horseman than I thought,' he said, shaking his head and chuckling at once.

'Diana came. And her brother. They're still up there. Come on, I'll explain on the way. Get in the ute.' I couldn't bear to start the telling or I thought I'd boil over. I whipped around and slid back through the still open door. Eric slotted in beside without a word. I started the engine but just as I changed gears Eric yelled, 'Hold on!' He jumped out, leaving the door ajar, and ran into the house.

'Where the hell are you going?' I screeched. They were done for. It would be too late.

A few minutes later Eric dashed back with a pile of blankets. Underneath he held two litre bottles of water. 'Somebody's got to think straight,' he said jumping back in and slamming the door.

I didn't move for a second.

'Wake up, you drongo. Drive like the clappers.'

I gunned the engine and we roared out the gate.

As the ute crested the first hill, I finally said, 'You know what she's like. Single-minded. She helped me catch the horses, but then her brother disappeared. She wouldn't leave.' I couldn't look at him, burning at this lame excuse. In the distance, yellow-grey smoke had settled over the pines like dead skin. Towards the south a blush showed that the fire was alive and greedy, hunting for them too.

Flare-Up

I leap two scabby logs and dodge a stump.
The path now seems more definite.
I'm almost at the clearing.
At least I might get my bearings there.

And then I hear a voice somewhere —
could it be Philip?
My heart flares and just as I shout, 'Here!'
I pitch face down into a mess of leaves —

dirt sprays in my mouth,
I spit and cough, roll over, catch my breath,
lie on my back, look up. Rub my eyes
until I'm seeing stars

or embers float across. The sky's like phlegm.
I struggle on my elbows, sit,
try to stand, collapse with pain
just as I hear another shout.

Hope flares as I rise again, then dies.
Nerves relay the truth —
something in my ankle's torn.
And I can't see what's caught alight nearby.

Conor: Dead Heat

I'm silent the rest of the way to the pine forest. Eric knows enough to let me simmer. But he's on his mobile to Alex, a mate in the CFS, asking where the fire is. When he says, 'More than one?' I feel my heart lurch. All at once I'm snap frozen like that time I was twelve and the lake ice gave way under me.

We park near the gate. Eric tosses me a water bottle and a blanket. 'For the fire. And in case someone's hurt.' He doesn't meet my eyes.

'Now what?' I grab his arm and plead. I suddenly realise that I don't have a clue how to search. I'm helpless here. Sweet Jesus (and all at once I wish I believed), how will I be any use?

But he's tapping his phone. 'SOS calls only now. Check yours.'

I slip mine out of my pocket and nod, 'Same thing. That means I can't ring Diana.'

'But you might be able to reach the CFS. We've been ordered to leave, but I told Alex that wasn't going to happen. He knows where we are and who's missing. They'll keep an eye out for your girl and her brother.'

He walks off fast so I trot to catch up. As soon as I reach his side he says, 'There's three fires. One serious and the other two – for now – only a distraction from the main event. But they've had to pull off blokes from that fight to keep the others in check. The bad one is pretty far south, but if the wind picks up again it might blow through the whole forest like a steam train.'

He unlatches the gate and we both push through tall grass. When I tell him which way Diana set off, he nods. 'OK, I'll head right, you go left after her. You don't have any notion where Philip went?'

I shake my head.

'Thought so. Cooee every five minutes as long as you can so we keep track of each other.' He barks out orders as if he were the trainer late for the races. Eric moves off but then stops to rummage in his pocket. He hands me a compass. 'Pa gave me this when we first camped in the Flinders. I know this forest. You don't. If you wind up lost, it'll be just my luck to get fried chasing after you too.'

Then the wind surges from the right, the direction Eric is going. Is it south or north? I have no sense of direction as the pines fold over us. What sky I can see looks diseased. I close my palm over the compass.

Already Eric is twenty feet away, bashing through the bush as if he's in a race. I'm the late starter hoping for more than a dead heat.

Echo

I'm crawling towards the light but then I see
only naked trunks, thick prison bars,
a line of pines that stop the track – dead.

The floor's a waste of needles
that crunch like almond shells under my knees.
I brush aside green tufts newly dropped.

I can't see any flare-ups here,
just flames of light that flicker through the trees.
I taste the air. There's too much of that smell

of antiseptic green now cauterised,
of eucalypts exploding –
that smothering aroma of fresh death.

My chest begins to smoulder as I stand
and yell, 'Stupid moll.
You've got no water.'

I throw my head back and howl again.
'Stupid! Stupid! Stupid!' till I'm hoarse.
The wind hurls 'Stupid' back into my face.

Conor: Flaming Mad

I trot off on the only scrappy trail I can see to the left. Bloody idiot isn't good enough for me. I should be flaming mad at myself, but all I feel now is flat, as if I've run my race and there's nothing left in the tank.

I walk smack into a tree. I must be in a daze, so swig water from the bottle Eric had the sense to bring and dab some on my skin where I can feel a bump swelling. I'm no use to anyone this way. I begin to focus now trying to see signs that someone's passed – snapped branches, boot tracks. I can't make out anything on the ground but gum leaves, pine needles and pellets of roo dung.

The only sounds I hear are the forest's shed skin crunching under my boots, the wind whining at my stupidity and suddenly, far off, a siren. The CFS? 'You're no tracker, lad,' I hear my father say in my head. 'But pull yourself together.'

I check the compass again and it tells me I'm still heading north by northeast.

And then I see it, a mark where the bark's been scraped off. A bit further ahead, I spot another and this one looks like a 'D.' I can't believe Diana had the sense to do that. She's left me a trail better than crumbs. I find three more but then the marks peter out thirty metres ahead. At least I've got some sense of her direction. I stop, take another swig of water, push on faster, feeling that this might turn out all right. The horses are safe and if I can just keep control – if I don't, I'll be lost too but then I won't care. I want us all out together, whole.

I hear Eric's first 'Cooee' far off to the right and bellow out my own till my throat flames. I keep hollering for a moment, with the wind at my back, hoping that it will carry my voice to her.

Once Upon a Time

Is the forest mocking me?
Was 'Stupid' thrown back in my face?
Have I gone mad with grief and guilt?
Will my ankle hold out? Should I just give up,
collapse in a heap, let smoke do its work?
Which way would be better to die?
To dissolve in the forest's smoky breath?
If flames really are hungry,
should I welcome their tongues,
let them lick what sweetness is left?
Once upon a time,
I longed to be weightless ash,
but the story was changing.
Now I want to rewrite the ending.

Conor: Cooee

The smoke's thick as autumn fog was over our lake in Ireland when I could hear the swans calling that it was time to fly south. They swirled above my head like ghosts. What do I wish? Not to be haunted, that's certain. The best shock would be Diana and Philip materialising out of that fire's bad breath as solid flesh and bone.

I've cooeed twice in the past ten minutes but no answer from Eric for at least half an hour. I find a gum with sturdy branches and hoist myself up till I can see more of the forest. It's hazy, though, enough to blur my vision and turn my stomach. Smoke pours into the putrid sky from the far right, as if a volcano's mouth was spewing. I hear more sirens but they're faint, telling me the battle is southeast. If it wasn't for Eric, I'd be lost good and proper.

I cooee again before I jump down, shuffling on my perch so my voice carries in each direction. Then I think I hear something to the left, leap out of the tree, find a gap in the brush and slip through, yelling 'Diana? Diana!'

Illusions

A magpie explodes out of a pine
but falls like floating embers.
Why is it here?
It flails along a branch
until I realise its leg has snapped –
no balance, then no chance.

The gale sucks in its breath –
a moment of silence for the living
and soon-to-be dead. But that's not us,
not me and Philip. I've decided
it's no time for grieving.
I find a branch for a walking stick

and hobble as I shout.
Once again the breeze begins to swell.
I hear my name stretched out in syllables.
It must be Philip.
'Di,' he shouts, 'I'm here.'
My heart finally knows it's here and now.

I limp till I see him waving madly.
We crash together like pathetic lovers
that the fates have crossed.
Philip's hyped and chatters on –
He's proud that he spotted smoke and foxes.
And did we save the horses?

I listen but don't talk, split for survival –
I'm the one who needs to lead us home.
This drama hasn't reached a climax yet.
Back in Oz the wizard let his hopefuls
choose their own illusions. On this day,
I'll take the illusion of fate, the fact of love.

Conor: Back from the Dead

I had Irish luck today. First Eric drove up in time to keep me from charging off alone. The only fires I knew about I'd seen on TV – blurred flashes of people running, kids crying, water arcing over flames three stories high. But nothing prepared me for this heat and smell – the forest like a giant panic room where we all were trapped, but couldn't hear each other.

Before I could pity myself more, I had another bit of luck. I heard calls. I checked Eric's compass and then pushed off, hollering too. The cooees grew louder. Suddenly, not twenty metres away, there they were, crashing through the pines, Diana screeching, 'Philip. That way. See Conor?' and Philip hauling his sister behind by the hand. He's six foot, that lad, and when he saw me he stomped on the pine needles so that they cracked like dry spaghetti. That made him laugh.

Although Diana was limping, trying to manoeuvre on a branch almost as tall as she was, she began laughing too. Then I couldn't help it, I snorted and shook my head, till we were all laughing and crying at the same time and it was hard to tell which came from tears or smoke.

As hot as it was Diana was shivering so I draped the blanket over her shoulders, clutched her hand and swung round to the path I'd followed. I had a fair idea now of which direction would lead us home. Philip wanted to be head scout so I let him bush-bash, telling him which way to turn.

Eric wasn't by the ute. I just hoped that he'd swung back away from the main fire. We waited another fifteen minutes but the smoke was thickening like scum over the trees and I was afraid we'd be well and truly trapped. I'd check with the CFS when I was home.

So we piled into the ute and raced the hell out of there, raced out of hell, laughing again as the wheels spun us right and left on that nubbly dirt, laughing because we'd come back from the dead.

Limbo

I sit in Conor's house and let him talk
although I can hear he's running down —
terror, tears and laughter made us drunk.
But this is a toxic kind of calm
that slaps your face to sober you at once.
I flood myself with water, then I float
on waves of tiredness. The taste of guilt
hasn't washed away. I watch the clock
and will the minute hand to melt and stick.
My brother is the only innocent.
His world, at least for now, will hardly change.
But mine and Conor's — have they shifted far?
This kitchen is a waiting room for hell.
No one moves or dares disturb the door.

Conor: Safe and Well

As soon as we're in my house we're drinking the best water I've ever tasted. We finished the bottle I had in the forest on the drive back and we're guzzling now from a two-litre flagon, passing it hand to hand. My throat shivers with the pleasure of coolness.

The phone rings and it's Father. He's been trying to reach me for hours. I have no sense of what time it is. I tell him we're all safe and well, the horses, Diana and her brother, although she needs to have her ankle checked out. He's says it's grand that Diana and I fetched Tequila and Hero. Even if the fire didn't reach to those fringe paddocks, the smoke, noise and wind might have driven them through a fence.

I tell him about Eric's blowout and how I was bloody lucky he came with me to search for Diana and Philip. I might still have been wandering around like our neighbour full of drink who always needs his wife to lead him home from the pub.

When Father asks where Eric is now, I have to admit that we lost track of him in the forest, but as soon as I hang up I'm calling his CFS mate to see if he's heard. If he says it's safe, I'll drive back to the forest gate in case Eric's waiting for me there before I head up to hospital.

'And if he isn't?' Father asks.

That's what I haven't dared face yet. For the moment all I do is breathe into the phone.

Calling

There are other calls to make,
but still we find we cannot rouse ourselves.
Philip slumps in his chair.

Conor stares as if my face is blank.
I feel like the eye of a storm,
full of deceptive calm.

We jump when the landline rings.
Conor's father again,
saying he'll do the feeds.

His son should stay in town as long as he needs.
When he hangs up, Conor shuts his eyes,
then opens them and punches Eric's number.

No answer. Out of range. Send a text.
Second try. Call Alex. Luck is with us.
He's within range, his unit's moving south.

But Conor's told in no uncertain terms
the forest's now off limits.
All adjacent roads are closed to traffic.

The CFS doesn't need more problems.
But Conor reminds him of another.
No one's heard from Eric.

No News

Finally I dare check my phone.
Five missed calls from Mum.
She must feel satisfied, I think —
she had a right to panic.

But someone's worked some magic.
When Conor calls for me,
assures her we're all fine, she believes.
The hospital's a sensible precaution.

Then I speak, only say, 'Hello,'
and wait for consequences. I'm surprised.
No accusations now, all that she wants
is confirmation that we both are whole.

Shame blocks my throat.
I'm not sure what has stolen my mum's voice.
Then Dad takes the phone
and tells me they'll be there in casualty.

Outside the heat gut-punches us.
The sky has been leached of any colour
except a rabid yellow.
Clouds form a pack and hunt each other.

We seek the safety of the ute.
Its air cools down and purrs Philip to sleep.
He curls into himself against the window.
I nuzzle into Conor, close my eyes

but can't lose consciousness.
I have to know. I tune the radio
as Conor's fingers graze across my thigh.
I hear a voice straining to sound tragic.

I hate clichés, those self-important words.
No news isn't always good.

Forecast

Casualty Notes copied by Robert Warren

Patient: Diana Warren
Age: 19
Presented with damage to left ankle.

Diagnosis:

> X-ray confirms no break.
> Torn ligament.

Treatment:
> elevation
> cold compress
> Panadeine Forte (RX).
> Ankle brace or strapping.
> Six weeks off riding.

Prognosis:
> Full recovery.

'You're young enough to heal completely.
A chance you might be vulnerable to strains
or weakness in the ankle.'
The doctor cheerfully predicts my future.
I'm not sure how far I'll ever see.
Still, I now agree
that some things can be fixed.
The trick, of course, is knowing what they are.

Bulletins from the Front

Strong northeasterlies that swing around.
Mature pine plantations. Too much fuel —
and too much hope. Too many true believers
living on the fringes of the forest.

I force myself to hear the body count.
A hobby farmer blasted in his barn.
A carbonised Madonna and her child
found huddled in a shed.

Someone mutters that it could be worse.
The camera pans as proof.
Six houses melted into memories
for those alive to have them.

A couple sheltered in a car survived.
We see what's left around them —
hectares of charcoal pencils smudge the sky.
And still none of us have heard from Eric.

Two horses wander blindly towards a dam.
Scorched sheep limp among the embers —
All need to be put down.
Who can pretend they have the heart?

With fences crisped like toast,
dairy cows are scattered through the paddocks,
wailing to be milked.
A few lucky crows decide to answer.

Flare-ups wink all night,
like nightmare flashbacks
infiltrate tomorrow.
Here only the television flickers

and heats my face as I realise
that while I muddled north searching for Philip,
shepherded by smoke,
the hungry fire hunted in the south.

Salvation

Afterlife at home.
While Philip is asleep,
yet again we endure the news.
Clean and cool, I know that I'm twice blessed.
But sour smoke, the ash of penances,
from this day on will flavour all my guilts –
and my betrayals, venial though they are.
Conor and I wonder about Eric.
Will we ever really know what happened?
And how much truth can any of us bear?

I make up the sofa bed for Conor
and say goodnight. We only dare to hug
but I still feel the pressure of his fingers.
I hesitate before I close my door.
I know parents can't absolve your sins,
but before I try to lose myself
in at least this night's oblivion,
I slip into her room, perch on the bed,
and testify to my long-suffering mother
I finally know what salvation means.

Conor: Father and Son

I crept away at dawn from Diana's house. I left a note saying I'd call that night, but I had to go back to help Father and to find out the truth. No need to expect the worst. It was easy to lie on paper. My gut felt cauterised.

Father had just finished the morning feeds and we sat and talked over our mugs of tea like we hadn't for years. Talked about nothing much at first: the abscess on Misty's hoof; the girth galls that Tequila had when she came to us; the boggy patches on the beach; the cost of feed. Neither of us wanted to work. We sat out under the back verandah, half in the shadows, listening to each other and the white noise of the flies. Eric hovered between us — or his absence — but we ignored it.

Then Father said, looking straight ahead at Quinn as he worried the latch on his yard, 'Tragedy rips you apart, but sometimes puts you back together.' Just like that, out of nowhere. Was Mother whispering in his ear again? But it wasn't only her I knew. The fire had spoken to him as well in a language he couldn't ignore. Smoke still suffocated the ridges to our left and the sky's blue was watered down to half strength.

'I've already called the CFS hotline to check on Eric. Still no word. And a lass named Mimi called. She asked for you.'

I felt that weakness in my muscles again; they didn't want to lift me up and walk me inside. But I swigged the last of my tea and went to find the number.

Mimi

Conor says that he spoke to Eric's girl.
She's going crazy. He doesn't answer his phone.

The only message she hears,
'The person you have called is not available.'

'That's not what he told me,
the first time that we met.'

Conor repeats her words,
wonders how she can joke.

'Did she laugh?' I ask.
'I didn't hear a sound.

I told her no one knows anything yet.
But somehow she sounded resigned,

as if she believed,
this is how life turns out.'

Before she hung up she said,
'Eric was the best bloke I ever had.'

Conor: Cool Change

A fresh southerly crept over the sand dunes at dusk and surprised Father and me while we chugged along in the tractor, tossing hay into the paddocks.

It took until the next afternoon, after water bombing, back burning, hosing and bagging, for the main fire to be declared under control. Hot spots would continue to sizzle and spit, the news reported, especially in inaccessible areas. When I drove to the fodder store on the other side of town, I could still see embers delicate as milkweed puffs floating in the distance as they did at home at the end of summer. Some CFS crews wouldn't be getting sleep any time soon, even though the temperature had dropped.

At eight that night the phone rang. As soon as I heard Alex say 'Conor,' I knew. He called it an accident, rotten luck, but then luck was everything when you were trying to outsmart a fire. They had found Eric about three kms from the entrance to the forest. He had covered a lot of ground quickly, even in that heat and against the wind.

This shouldn't have happened to Eric, I thought. But it did and I never could change that.

Alex said that it looked as if a falling branch had flattened him. Had he woken up at all? If he had, the smoke would probably have been too thick for him to know where he was. But the fire knew. The cool change came too late for him.

Whispers and Prayers

I hobble up the path on Conor's arm
following the coffin.
An uncle has decided something simple,
just a graveside service, cheap and quick.
Eric has no parents who can mourn him.
The uncle has a swatch of silver hair
and looks as if he enjoys his beer.
'We seem to die young in my family.
Eric's parents, Jennifer, my wife,
and then our only daughter.
I don't know why I'm the one still left,'
we hear him whisper to a stocky girl.

What can she say to that?
'Mimi,' I breathe into Conor's ear.
'That must be her.' I judge her from the rear.
She's built for comfort and her stormy curls,
though caught up in a band,
refuse to be disciplined in grief.
And when she moves around the grave,
comfort is the last thing I see.
Her face is frighteningly still,
as if she has decided not to feel
anything again. I understand
too well that wish to be untouchable.

We interlace our fingers and I squeeze
Conor's hand so hard my silver rings
dig in. The chaplain mumbles empty words.
The ashen sky reminds us all of dust.
What's done is done and yet no one moves.
Then Mimi stirs, fishes in a pocket
and fills her hand with blossoms,
flags of scarlet petals that she waves
into the final darkness. But the sun

flames, reminding us that we are living.
I pray to whoever might be listening,
'Please forgive what might need forgiving.'

Conor: Afternoon

Another red alert day. At dawn the wind still thrashed like a cat caught by its tail, but by noon it only purred. The sun wasn't giving away an inch of the sky. One pm. Two pm. The hours had no energy left to limp any faster.

Father and I sat, simmering in the house, with no will to think or do. Then he rose, got more water from the fridge, and handed me the bottle. 'We could always sell up …' His eyes dared me to answer.

I swigged another mouthful. My phone was a dead weight on my belt, reminding me of everything that Diana and I still hadn't said. I didn't want to run away now from the saying.

'Would you come?' His voice, dampened by heat, had no energy left either.

I swallowed more water, let my insides cool down and stood. 'Or, we could always buy an air conditioner, like everyone else we know with any sense.'

Father laughed so loud he scared that visiting ginger Tom off the kitchen windowsill. Then he grabbed his hat and tilted his head at me.

'Let's feed up early and go for a swim,' he said, still chuckling as if the cool change had come through.

Normal

Two weeks have passed and yet I somehow feel
as if I've always lived at Conor's place.
Today's a normal day. We wake, make love,
gulp down cups of tea, eat toast and jam,
stack the dishes and then set to work
exercising three or four young horses
before the heat sets in and stops the clock.
We just have energy to wash them down,
let them roll, rug them, make the feeds.

At ten am more tea with Conor's father
as we talk about the training schedules.
We sit underneath the front verandah,
half-blinded by the light, that shimmering
that rises from the land and moves in waves
across the sun-scorched paddocks to the sea.
I ask myself what's normal now. Just this?
Just sleep, wake, love, eat, talk,
work, ride, sweat, and sometimes plan –
those details that move me through the day.

Because the other thing I know is grief,
a bedmate too that shares our tangled sheets.
But then there's joy, which flickers through our days
and blinds us to ourselves even at night.
What's normal? I realise no one can say,
not when you spy into people's heads,
and see the backdrop of their every days,
hear that voice that tells them what to hate
and hopefully to love. One thing I feel:
our silent bodies sometimes speak the truth.

Conor: Laying Ghosts to Rest

Eric's been laid to rest, but ghosts still rustle through my dreams. Maybe I've been fooling myself, it's not just Father who's tied to the past. And now I have more ghosts that need appeasing.

Diana and I talk late into the night in my bed. We agree that what happened is really no one's fault and yet that day haunts us. It's hard to fight against something you can't see, something that follows you like a shadow, but when you turn around it spins away. That sharing of guilt makes me want her more. Sometimes it lies between us and sometimes we can't pull apart, as if we were magnetised.

We both need to make decisions, but look for excuses. Tiredness rolls in like fog and we wake to an insistent sun and birds tap dancing on the roof. The phone rings and rings, reminding me of everything that needs doing. The yarded horses whinny and clang their gates for breakfast. They don't care about doubts or fears.

Our bodies make their own decisions, raise us up and move us on.

Riding for the Disabled

The first time I drove him
to RDA in the hills
Philip packed his pastels,
his talisman, a rearing plastic stallion,
apples 'to make the new horse like me' –
and that was all it took to fall in love.

And now he understands
why I need to ride.
Now he also wants the real thing,
gives himself to rhythm –
the four-beat walk –
the feel of harmony.

But that's not all. One morning
when we stop to buy new season's apples,
Jonathans for his favourite horse,
Long John with a silver tail –
he hands me one and smiles.
'I can tell you something you don't know.'

'There's plenty I don't know.'

He shakes his head and reaches for my arm.
He won't play this game.
'What does my name mean?'

I halt, foursquare,
an apple halfway to my mouth,
admit I have no clue.

'You see?
That's what I learned from my instructor.
It's why I need to ride.'

At last, his face beams,
I got what I wished for.
He wants to savour that he knows, I don't,
but can't resist sharing in the secret,
mysterious as chocolate
hiding a surprise.

'Philip is my name –
lover of horses.'

Conor: Home Country

It's time, that's what I told him. Years ago he ran away, couldn't bear to walk on the earth we put her under. He hauled me with him. When we left, insects were beginning to whirr and click, larches and oaks were breaking out in leaves as if spring was a green sickness, but I didn't want to be cured. The ashes grew full of themselves, curling out like Mother's hair.

Her garden looked its best then, as if having her in the little churchyard across the lake soothed it after our neglect. That last week while we packed, soft June rain misted down, but by midday the sun always shouldered aside the clouds, stamping its warmth on everything. I remember standing near an oak with ivy snaking up its trunk, the garden's breath evaporating in the air.

But the irises still glistened, their wet petals a faded purple bruise, and the slick green stems of the yellow and white tulips. They were crowded next to the lavender, which Mother dried and tied into bags for her drawers. There were plump fuchsia, red like Japanese lanterns, and pots of geraniums, clusters of salmon and pink, whose rough leaves felt like tongues and smelled like sweat. It seemed new now that we were going, the magenta bells of the foxgloves ringing with bees. All of it shifted and glowed as if I was seeing it through wavy glass. That last day before sleep I stood by the back door inhaling the garden's perfume till I felt sick with it.

It's time for us both. I told him I'd already booked the tickets. Father knew I was lying, I wouldn't have the money on my own, but he let the falsehood stick, a kind of glue between us, binding us to this dangerous journey back.

So now after dinner we plan what we'll do. Go to the races, see the odd cousin, tour around the old property like strangers, criticise the new owners, wade in the lake, watching our corpse-pale legs shiver the water. When I was a lad Father told me that a lake was like life. Fickle, warm and cold in spots, but you had to keep swimming if you wanted to reach the far side.

Then when Father's ready we'll visit Mother, place a bunch of flowers on her stone — sweet-corn yellow daffodils, if we can buy them in winter, leave her to feed the land she'd never have left.

Diana is staying for us. For her. She'll look after things, keep the new apprentice in check, and the neighbour will help. She's so quick sometimes it scares me. I thought I was shoving facts down her throat, like a goose being fattened, but she gobbled it all and always seemed hungry. Whatever we mean to each other, the horses mean too, maybe more. But I don't mind. We'll see.

That's what she says. Let things ride. And she's right. The horses could use a spell, especially in this fierce summer. We all need a spell. Finished with school, we can wait a year or so and then plan. Maybe more study for her, maybe even some day for me. But the horses come first. For now.

And that's what we'll come back to. Our horses and this temperamental land where nothing's taken for granted, where you can't bet on the weather to be on your side, where the heat seeps into your blood so that the horizon throbs at dusk in your head. Where anything green that shoots up after a shower thrills like a dark horse that comes in. You don't collect your winnings yet. But you work and hope. Nothing's for free. That teaches you not to let guilt numb your senses and waste what you have.

Diana's learned that lesson too. And when I return? But she told me not to think about that. Just come home, she said. That's easy. I know what it means to be home.

Good Works

I head for the front paddock,
parallel to the road.
Grazed down last month
it's spiking up again
like Philip's three-day growth.

Conor's father gave me this advice:
'Get them used to noise —
passing traffic and the neighbour's cattle.
Make it all familiar. Helps them settle
once they finally travel to the track.

When it's hot and crowded,
with squealing horses, owners barking orders,
while the trainers try to park their trucks,
you could be in
the waiting room to Hell.'

I asked him, 'Where's the gate that leads to Heaven?'
He laughed and shooed me off.
'Just do good works,
that's what our priest would say.
So go and do some now.'

I let young Hero stretch,
scratch his muzzle with a rear hoof,
then talk him past the scary chicken coop,
the clapped-out cars, the hoses,
sunning like black snakes across our path.

This is my work
and I am good at it.
I thank whatever nameless gods there are
for giving me
good work to finally do.

Racing the Kangaroo Island Bus

The bus drones in the distance
like a shark patrol scanning the coast.
But the road's empty as I gallop past,
gums and pines guarding the fence.

Just as we wheel around again
the KI bus enters the race,
audience glued to the glass,
snapping their final memories.

Then there's me and my horse —
we streak past the bus,
a pulse of bronze and blue,
flashing between the trees as the sun sets.

Some point and click
this last glimpse of country.
Horse and human — whoosh and blink —
who was that? No matter.

Now we will always be
that fleeting thought
looping through someone's mind,
grasped, then gone.

And we are still moving
together into the dark.
We love these moments
when muscles stretch out,

everything fluid and free
in our endless circle.
It's what we are for
in the time we have left.

No one else needs to know
who, why or how.
We're here
               here
                     now.

Coda

Losing It – Reprise

You never finished that story.

'Can there be a proper ending
when I never really began?'

Too clever for your own good.
You don't fool me.

'So who are you?'

You know. You care.

'I've only just discovered
what care means.'

Sentimental slop.

'Then let me wallow.'

You'll drown. Look.
Feel our body bloat.

'I'll prick it with my pen
and you can hiss.'

'Losing it' is lost.

'But something's saved.
Even after fires, in the ashes
fragments of a life can glimmer through.'

Fool's gold, if you ask me.

'Who's asking you? You're the one who's lost.'

That's wishful thinking.
You can never change.

'I can wish –
Philip's in my head, his wizard's voice,
saying "Hocus-pocus. Scat. Just vanish."'

And so I choose the voice I want to answer.
There might be ashes on my tongue,
but also sweet tastes from lazy dreams
and from my past.

Clara, sister-lover,
still gallops in my veins.
Mariska sighs and tells me I am lovely.
And Gran? She always jokes.
She's the one I know will keep me honest.

But the fire taught me one more lesson,
the one I can't ignore –
how easily your hopes
can be consumed.

Why would I want to finish?
In this new year one thing I finally know –
I'm only learning now
what losing means.

A Sort of Hymn

This body is my body.
I reclaim the living me.

The one that rides horse-high, braving the wind.
The one that sweats and smells, enjoying rapture,
singly and together, loving its skin.
The one that lusts for food it sometimes hates,
that shrinks and swells following the moon.
A body that feels power in every fibre.

Body, my self, my own,
my humble house,
this is my promise to you,
the slate I wipe clean.

I'll live and learn through you.
If I dare and damage,
I'll master how to repair,
proud of my scars.

Imperfect miracle
of flesh and bone,
wherever you are or will be,
you are my home.

Notes

The Legend of the Seven Sisters

'Myths and Legends': This poem refers to the West Australian version as told in May L O'Brien, *The Story of the Seven Sisters,* illustrated by Sue Wyatt, Canberra: Aboriginal Studies Press, 1999.

'Rereading': This poem refers to the version of the myth discussed in *Listen to Ngarrindjeri Women Speaking: Kungun Ngarrindjeri Miminar Yunnan,* edited by Diane Bell for the Ngarrindjeri Nation, North Melbourne: Spinifex Press, 2008, 29-34. Bell cites this story and makes it clear that it is David Unaipon's narration. Also see the 2014 edition of Bell's 1998 book, *Ngarrindjeri Wurruwarrin: A world that is, was, and will be,* Melbourne: Spinifex Press. Bell says that 'Unaipon uses *Yartooka,* while current orthography uses *yartuka*' (email 27.7.14).

> ...when it gets cold, that's when they disappear from the sky. Then they come back down and go under the water to be with their mother. Their mother belonged to the Warrior Women of the Island (29).

> *Yartooka* [young girls], we have passed through the testings our Elders had prescribed and suffered much pain... You must know that the selfish person is not happy, because he thinks only of himself. ...Greed and pain and fear are caused by thinking too much of self, and so it is necessary to vanquish them. Will you not go and do as we have done (32)?

> The Great Spirit was so pleased with them that he sent a great Star Spirit, and the *Yartooka* were transferred to the heavens without death...(32).

Quotations from *The Wizard of Oz* appear in L Frank Baum, *The Wizard of Oz*, Harmondsworth and New York: Puffin Books, 1985.

'Firewater': Epigraph from Chapter 12, 'The Search for the Wicked Witch,' 94.
'Megaheart': Epigraph from Chapter 5, 'The Rescue of the Tin Woodman,' 39-40.

Quotations from *Alice in Wonderland* appear in Lewis Carroll, *Alice in Wonderland & Through the Looking Glass*, illustrated by John Tenniel, Kingsport: Grosset & Dunlap, 1946.

'Philip: The Last Tea Party': Epigraph from Chapter 7, 'A Mad Tea Party,' 81, 75.
'A Pack of Cards': Epigraph from Chapter 12, 'Alice's Evidence,' 137.
'Going Off': Epigraph from Chapter 12, 'Alice's Evidence,' 137.

John Donne: 'Desire': 'We're tapers too, and at our own cost die.'
See 'The Canonization' and other poems by Donne. Edited editions note the seventeenth-century pun on 'die' (to reach orgasm and to lose some of one's life essence).

'Library: Passion and Ideals': See Peter Shaffer, *Equus*, Harlow: Pearson Education Limited, 1993.

'Hello darkness, my old friend/I've come to talk with you again': These are the first two lines of a song, 'The Sounds of Silence,' written by Paul Simon and recorded by Paul Simon and Art Garfunkel in 1964 for their first album, *Wednesday Morning, 3AM* (Columbia Records), but then remixed for their second album, *The Sounds of Silence* (1966).

Acknowledgements

The author is deeply gratefully for a Varuna Writer's Residential Fellowship (2009), an Arts SA Professional Development Grant (2009) and a Varuna International Exchange Residency at the Tyrone Guthrie Centre in Annaghmakerrig, Ireland (2005), without which she could not have written *Vanishing Point*.

My sincere thanks to Professor Leslie Jacobson, of the Department of Theatre and Dance at George Washington University, who is also the Founding Artistic Director of Horizons Theatre, the oldest feminist theatre in the United States. Our collaboration began with the workshopping of a script based on *Vanishing Point* in 2009 with Horizon actors and GW students. All the staged readings of *Vanishing Point* to date, including the production at the Kennedy Center for the Performing Arts 10th 'Page to Stage' Festival (Millennium Stage South) in September 2011, and the two-week workshop/performance in June 2012, have been directed by her as well.

A sequence from *Vanishing Point* was runner up for the 2006 Josephine Ulrick $10,000 Poetry Prize.

A poem under the title 'An Anorexic Testifies' was shortlisted for the 2009 Rosemary Dobson Poetry Prize and appeared on the prize website.

A version of 'Lesson on Bones' appeared in *Blue Dog: Australian Poetry* as 'Bones: An Anorexic's Hymn,' Vol. 5, No. 10, November, 2006: 17-18.

'Climate Change,' a sequence from this work (including prose and poems), appeared in Donna Lee Brien, Nigel Krauth & Jen Webb (eds) 2010 *The ERA Era: Creative writing as research, TEXT Special Issue 7*, October: 1–6 http://www.textjournal. com.au.

The first two sections of 'First Love' (i Changeling and ii First Flight) appeared in *A Cadence of Hooves: A Celebration of Horses*, Igo, CA: Yarroway Mountain Press, 2008: 199–202.

'Baptism' (part 2) of 'Namesake,' an extract from 'Epilogue' and an extract from 'Rereading' appeared in Jeri Kroll, 'From *now* to *once upon a time*: Reading the Book of Myths' (paper from the Icarus Extended Panel – a textual/sexual intervention), in the Strange Bedfellows Or Perfect Partners Papers: The Refereed Proceedings of the 15th Conference of the Australasian Association of Writing Programs, 2010. See http://www.aawp.org.au/the_strange_bedfellows_or_perfect_partners.

A selection of poems from *Vanishing Point* appeared in Jeri Kroll, *Workshopping the Heart: New and Selected Poems*, Adelaide: Wakefield Press, 2013, 180-205.

www.ingramcontent.com/pod-product-compliance
Lightning Source LLC
Chambersburg PA
CBHW021003260626
47169CB00006B/1915